'Why don't you take a day off?'

Olivia shook her head.

'Well, at the very least have a lie-in. Come in a bit later—we'll manage.'

'I couldn't do that. I've got this frightful boss, you see. You wouldn't believe the fuss he makes.'

Clem laughed. 'I really am sorry about this morning. I can't promise it won't happen again, but I will try. I don't ever want to make a promise to you and break it.'

The strangest thing considering her total distrust in men, was that she really believed him.

He moved towards her again, all the time gazing deeply into her eyes. There was no mistaking his intention. He was going to kiss her properly. She could feel her pulse pounding in her temples as his warm hands tenderly cupped her face. But before his full, sensual lips met hers, the urgent sound of his pager rudely interrupted the moment.

Carol Marinelli did her nursing training in England and then worked for a number of years in Casualty. A holiday romance while backpacking led to her marriage and emigration to Australia. Eight years and three children later, the romance continues…

Today she considers both England and Australia her home. The sudden death of her father prompted a reappraisal of her life's goals and inspired her to tackle romance writing seriously.

THE OUTBACK NURSE

BY
CAROL MARINELLI

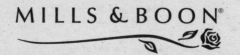

MILLS & BOON®

For Dad, with love always.

First published in Great Britain 2001
Harlequin Mills & Boon Limited,
Eton House, 18-24 Paradise Road, Richmond, Surrey TW9 1SR

© Carol Marinelli 2001

ISBN 0 263 82678 3

Set in Times Roman 10½ on 11½ pt.
03-0701-53705

Printed and bound in Spain
by Litografía Rosés, S.A., Barcelona

CHAPTER ONE

'BUT there must be some other work—anything?' Olivia fought for control, trying to keep the note of panic from her voice.

'Ms Morrell, we have plenty of work on our books, particularly for someone with your casualty experience. However, as you've said you will only consider a live-in position, it makes things very difficult. Even the large teaching hospitals are cutting back on their living accommodation—the agency nurses just don't get a look-in.'

Olivia nodded. She had heard it all before. This was the fifth agency she had tried and the only one that had actually come up with a job—a live-in position nursing a recently disabled gentleman in Melbourne. The work in itself didn't worry her, but in her present emotional state Olivia doubted if she would be much good at bolstering the young man's spirits.

'Well, thank you for your time.' Olivia stood up, smoothing her smart grey skirt. Trying to blink back the ever-threatening tears, she reached for her bag. 'If anything comes in, you will let me know?'

Miss Lever looked up from the files she was half-heartedly flicking through. Suddenly she felt sorry for Olivia for despite the designer clothes, immaculate hair and make-up she obviously wasn't as together as she first appeared.

'Just a moment.' Miss Lever tapped the keyboard of her computer. 'I'm sure this won't remotely interest you, but I did receive an e-mail today from our New South Wales office. It would seem they're having trouble filling a particular vacancy. It is live-in, but I can't imagine....' Her voice trailed off as she printed off the particulars.

'Tell me about it,' Olivia said sitting down sharply. Surely there must be a job for her.

'The position is for a charge nurse with advanced nursing skills to work in general practice.'

'It sounds perfect.' Olivia nodded enthusiastically.

'I think you'd better let me fill you in a bit before you go getting too excited. The practice is in Kirrijong—have you heard of it?'

Olivia nodded. 'Vaguely. It's way out in the bush, isn't it?'

'That's an understatement. It's very pretty apparently, but also very isolated. The practice covers a vast area and the surrounding townships. But when I say "surrounding", you could hardly say they're close by. Kirrijong isn't close to anything. They're actually in the process of building a small cottage hospital to service the area, which is due for completion in three to six months. The position is available until then, but if you like it...' Miss Lever gave a cynical smile '...I'm sure they'd be delighted to keep you on.'

She looked over at Olivia, expecting to see a look of horror on the well-made-up face. This was, after all, no modern city surgery. Instead, she was surprised to see Olivia closely reading the e-mail, her face full of interest. Perhaps she would get her commission after all. 'You did your midwifery training in England, I see, as well as your general training.'

'Yes, but I came straight out to Australia afterwards, and I've been in Casualty ever since. Apart from the odd surprise delivery in the department, I haven't practised.'

Miss Lever shrugged. 'They only say midwifery training desirable. You're more than qualified and, anyway, they're desperate.'

'What do you mean?'

'Well...' Miss Lever shuffled uncomfortably in her seat. 'Look, I'm not aware of your circumstances and, of course, it's none of my business, though it does appear you need a live-in job in a hurry.'

Olivia blushed. Was it that obvious how desperate she was?

'I just feel I should emphasise this is not the sort of job you're used to. Apart from your regular hours, you will be expected to help out in emergencies at any given time. It's an extremely busy surgery, with a large, complicated patient list. A lot of procedures that in the city would be done in a hospital are undertaken there.'

'Would I be the only nurse in the practice?'

'Yes, and if there's a seriously ill patient there will be no cardiac arrest team to bleep, no surgeons waiting scrubbed up in Theatre. Just you and the good doctor until the road or air ambulance arrives, and that can take a long time.' She paused a moment, before continuing, 'I ought to tell you that by all accounts Dr Clemson isn't the most pleasant of personalities.'

'In what way?'

Miss Lever leant over her desk and lowered her voice. 'Well, according to the last two girls sent there—who, incidentally, only managed two weeks between them—Dr Clemson is recently widowed and extremely bitter. He's supposedly very moody and demanding.'

Olivia let out a sigh of relief. For a moment she had thought Miss Lever was going to say he had made a pass at the other nurses. The very last thing she needed right now was to be stuck in the middle of nowhere with an elderly doctor and his roving hands.

'That doesn't worry you?'

'I've had more than my share of moody, difficult doctors, I can assure you. I'm not going to collapse in a heap if he barks at me. I can give as good as I get. As long as Dr Clemson can cope with that, I can manage his tantrums.'

Miss Lever looked at Olivia's determined face and the fiery red hair. She had no doubt she could.

'You sound as if you don't want me to take the position,' Olivia added.

'On the contrary...' Miss Lever smiled '...I just want to be sure you know what you're letting yourself in for. I'm not too keen on being on the receiving end of the formidable Dr Clemson's temper if I send someone unsuitable. I actually think you'll do very well—you've got a marvellous résumé. Three years in charge of such a busy casualty department must prepare you for just about any eventuality.'

'Just about,' Olivia agreed.

'Look, why don't I go and rustle up some coffee and leave you on your own for a few minutes to think it over?'

'Thank you, I'd appreciate that.'

Miss Lever walked to the door and, turning to ask how Olivia took her coffee, thought better of it, seeing her brimming eyes as she fished in her bag for a handkerchief. Closing the door quietly behind her, she shook her head. It was most unlike Miss Lever to put someone off a job— usually she was just interested in the commission. But there was something about Ms Morrell, a vulnerability behind that rather brittle exterior that made you not want to add to her troubles. She obviously had enough already.

Olivia leant back in the chair glad to be alone. Under normal circumstances she'd have had hysterics at the thought of a job out in the bush, with only a bitter old doctor as her colleague. But, then, who'd have thought, she reflected, she'd ever be in this situation, practically begging for a job? Sister Olivia Morrell, always so immaculate and in control. How happy she had been—a job she'd loved, Unit Manager in the emergency department at Melbourne

City Hospital, wonderful friends and, to cap it all, engaged to Jeremy Forster, Surgical Registrar, dashing, successful and good-looking.

Closing her eyes for a second, Olivia flashed back to the fateful day when Jessica, a dear friend and trusted colleague, had come into her office and asked for a private talk. How clearly she remembered the disbelief and horror as Jessica had gently told her that Jeremy was having an affair with his intern, Lydia Colletti.

At first Olivia had thought it must have been some sort of sick joke, a ghastly mistake, but, seeing the pain in her friend's eyes, she'd known she'd been hearing the truth. Looking back, it all seemed so obvious. Jeremy's mood swings, the exhaustion, the constant criticism. She had put it all down to the pressure of his work. He was due for a promotion soon to junior consultant and the competition was stiff. If they could just get through this, she had reasoned, surely he would be happier?

To add insult to injury, despite knowing the long hours and close proximity Jeremy shared with Lydia, she had never once felt threatened. She had trusted him. What a fool, what a stupid trusting fool.

Painfully, Olivia recalled their final row. She had confronted him, of course, and he'd sung like a bird, telling her in all too great a detail her faults, but Olivia had refused to take the blame for his infidelity.

'How could you do this Jeremy? How could you make love to her and then me?' she demanded, but Jeremy was unrepentant.

'Oh, come on, Olivia, when did we last make love? Our sex life is practically non-existent.'

'And that's supposed to be my fault?' she shouted, her anger welling to the surface. 'It's you who's always too tired or too busy. And now I know why, don't I? You were too damned exhausted after being with Lydia!'

'Well, at least she enjoys it Olivia. With you it's like making love to a skeleton, and about as lively.' He spat the words at her, his guilt and desire to end the discussion making him brutal.

Until finally, exhausted and reeling, all that was left to do was to throw a few hastily grabbed items into a bag and get out with as much dignity as she could muster, desperate to put some space between them.

It seemed that everyone except her had known about the affair. She couldn't go back to face the sympathetic stares and embarrassed silences. The only solution was to hand in her notice, which unfortunately meant surrendering the city apartment she leased from the hospital. Jessica's spare room provided a welcome haven but they both knew it was only temporary.

'Sorry I've been so long.' Miss Lever placed a cup and saucer on the desk in front of her and Olivia forced a smile, suddenly remembering where she was.

'I took the liberty of ringing Dr Clemson and telling him about you. You are still interested, I hope?'

Olivia nodded.

'Good. He was very keen.'

Olivia took a deep breath. 'How soon would he want me to start?'

'How soon can you get there?'

Hauling her suitcases off the train onto the platform, Olivia noticed she was the only passenger getting off at Kirrijong. In fact, the train only passed through once a day. Not for the first time, it hit her just how isolated she was. Gradually the city and suburbs had faded into endless bush, the lush green grass paling into sunburnt straw, acre after acre of dry cracked land. She had heard how the drought and dry winter had affected the farmers but, seeing for herself the parched bush and emaciated livestock, it made her realise the drought was far more than just a news bulletin or a page in the newspaper. Times were really tough here.

'G'day there, I'll get these. You must be Sister Morrell,' a friendly, sun-battered face greeted her, his eyes squinting in the setting sun. 'Jeez, how many cases have you got?'

Olivia blushed. It did seem a bit excessive, yet most of her clothes were still back at home. Throwing caution to the wind, Olivia had sold the car Jeremy had bought her as an engagement present, freeing up some cash. Jeremy would be furious. Blowing some money on a wardrobe more suited to the bush than her designer Melbourne gear had been a good tonic, at least for an afternoon.

Olivia was slightly taken back by the warmth of the man's welcome, having expected, from Miss Lever's description, a far more aloof greeting. Judging him to be in his mid-fifties, wearing dirty jeans and faded checked shirt, with a battered akubra shielding his face, Dr Clemson certainly didn't look the ogre Miss Lever had predicted. 'It's a pleasure to meet you, Dr Clemson.' She offered her hand, startled when he started to laugh.

'Youse didn't think I was the doctor? I can't wait to tell the missus. I'm Dougie, Dougie Kendall. My wife Ruby is Clem's housekeeper. I do a few odd jobs around the place, help out with the land.' He started to laugh again.

Olivia seethed. Did he really find it so funny? It was an obvious mistake. 'Well, Mr Kendall,' she said evenly, 'it's a pleasure to meet you.' It wouldn't do to get the locals offside quite so early.

Climbing into his dusty ute, Olivia winced as Dougie carelessly threw her expensive suitcases in the back. All the windows were wound down, forcing her to shout responses to Dougie's continual chatter. He pointed out the various residences as he hurtled the ute at breakneck speed along the dry, dusty road.

'That there belongs to the Hunts, a beaut family. Just had

a baby, a little fella, so no doubt youse'll be seeing them soon. And the land from now till the crossroads belongs to the Rosses.'

Olivia looked at the vast acreage and huge brick residence, far more formal than the weatherboard homes they had passed.

'They own a lot of land—mind, not as much as the doctor. Their daughter Charlotte is a model, well, that's what she calls herself anyway, I could think of a few other things.' He looked over at her, awaiting a response, but Olivia didn't rise to the bait. She wasn't interested in gossip. 'Charlotte's forever flitting in and out. One minute London the next Italy. She's supposed to be living in Sydney, but manages to put in an appearance here often enough and grace us with her presence. She's out with the doctor tonight—that's why he couldn't meet you.'

'Really?' Despite her earlier disinterest, Olivia sat up, suddenly intrigued. How rude. Surely he could have taken a night off from romancing someone young enough to be his daughter to welcome a new colleague.

'It's no business of mine, but she's a bit touched.' Dougie tapped his head and laughed. 'Clem wanted to come and meet youse himself but Charlotte rang with yet another "emergency" and of course he ends up running off to sort her out. Charlotte's a bit of a drama queen, if you know what I mean.'

Olivia knew what he meant all right. Wasn't that Lydia's game? Playing the helpless female, waiting for Jeremy to dash to her rescue. Olivia swallowed hard. While she had been bending over backwards to make their relationship work he had been rushing around comforting Lydia for every trivial hiccup or imagined problem that came her way.

'We're coming up to the surgery now.'

Night seemed to have fallen in a moment, with no dusk

to ease it in. Through the darkness Olivia could make out a huge rambling federation-style house with an array of plants hanging from the turned veranda posts. Dougie drove slowly past, the ute crunching on the gravel driveway. 'That's the doctor's house. The front of it is the surgery and he lives in the back part—it's pretty big.' He drove on for a couple more minutes and brought the truck to a halt. 'This is you.' He gestured to a pretty weatherboard with a huge veranda. The same array of hanging plants and terracotta pots adorned the entry and a wicker rocking chair sat idle in the front.

'Just for me?'

'Yep, all yours. My wife will be in through the week to take care of the cleaning and laundry. She'll show youse the ropes better than I can.'

'There's really no need. I can manage my own cleaning. I'm quite capable—'

'Sister,' he interrupted, 'youse'll be busy enough without running around doing housework. Anyway, don't be doing me missus out of a job.' He spoke roughly but his eyes were smiling.

'Oh, well, if you put it like that,' Olivia replied.

Dougie brought in her luggage as Olivia inspected 'home', her shoes echoing on the gorgeous jarrah polished floorboards that ran the length of the house. The lounge was inviting with two soft cream sofas littered with scatter cushions and a huge cream rug adding warmth to the cold floor. Someone thoughtful had arranged a bowl of burgundy proteas on the heavy wooden coffee-table. A huge open fireplace caught her eye. Olivia doubted whether she'd need it for, though dark outside, the air still hung heavy and warm.

'There's some red gum chopped. Ruby will set a fire up for you tomorrow. It still being spring, we get the odd chilly evening, though not for much longer. There's a fan heater in the kitchen cupboard, youse'll need that in the morning to take the chill off.'

Olivia smiled. 'It's a lovely house, beautifully decorated.'

'That was Kathy's work.'

'Kathy?' Olivia questioned.

'Yep, Kathy—Clem's wife, or rather late wife. She loved decorating. Spent weeks on this place, painting, stencilling, finding bits of furniture here and there.'

He spoke in the same casual manner but Olivia could hear the emotion in his voice.

'Anyway…' he gestured to the kitchen '…there's plenty in the fridge and cupboards to get you started. Ruby will be over in the morning to take you to the surgery. We don't want you feeling awkward on your first day.'

'Thank you, that's very kind.'

Dougie waved his hand dismissively. 'No worries. I'll leave youse to get settled in but, mind, if you need anything there's our number by the phone in the kitchen.' With a cheery wave he was off.

Olivia noticed he didn't even close the front door, just the flyscreen. This obviously wasn't the city, but old habits died hard. Olivia closed the door and turned the catch. A pang of homesickness hit her but, determined not to feel sorry for herself, she set about unpacking, until finally, with every last thing put away, she put the suitcases into the study wardrobe. This was home for now.

Peering in the fridge, Olivia smiled. There was enough food to last a month—a dozen eggs, bacon as thick as steak, milk, cheese. The pantry was just as well stocked. Tackling the Aga, Olivia put the kettle on. She'd earned a cup of tea and then she'd go straight to bed. The day seemed to have caught up with her all of a sudden.

A sharp knock on the door made her jump. Glancing at the clock, she saw it was edging on ten. Tentatively she opened the heavy door. Leaving the flyscreen closed, she peered at the large figure outlined in the darkness, trying to sound assured. 'Can I help you?'

'Olivia?'

'You are…' she said questioningly.

'Jake Clemson, but everyone calls me Clem.'

Olivia blushed, fumbling with the catch. 'Please, come in.' He was her new boss and she was treating him like some madman from the bush.

'I didn't mean to scare you.' He shook her hand firmly. 'Welcome to Kirrijong.'

Olivia smiled, taken aback not only by the unexpected friendliness but also by his appearance. Why had she assumed he'd be older? The man standing before her must only be in his thirties. She had imagined some austere, elderly doctor in tweeds. Jake Clemson, standing well over six feet, with battered jeans and an equally well-worn denim shirt, certainly didn't fit the image she'd had of him. His dark curly hair needed a good cut—he looked more like an overgrown medical student than a GP.

'I had hoped to meet you myself, but something came up.'

Olivia shrugged. If she had been expecting an apology or even an explanation she obviously wasn't going to get one. 'No problem. Mr Kendall was very helpful.'

'Dougie's a great bloke. I knew he'd take care of you.' He peered over her shoulder into the living room. 'Time for a quick chat?'

Olivia blushed again, suddenly feeling very rude. 'Of course. Come through—this way.' It was his house. As if he wouldn't know where the lounge was she thought feeling silly, but he just smiled.

'If I know Dougie and Ruby, there'll be a few stubbies in the fridge. Do you fancy one?'

Nodding, she followed him into the kitchen as he casually opened the fridge and helped himself to the beer.

Opening two stubbies, he made his way back to the living room. Obviously, if she wanted a glass she'd better get it herself!

'So how do you feel about coming to work here?' he asked in a deep, confident voice with only a hint of an Australian accent.

Olivia busied herself pouring the beer and managing to spill most of it. 'I'm really looking forward to it,' she lied. She could hardly tell him she was having a full-on panic attack and wondering what on earth had possessed her. 'The agency gave me quite an extensive brief. It all sounds very interesting, though I wish I had a bit more midwifery experience.'

He stared at her, taking in her slender frame and long red hair. The cheerful, confident voice belied her body language. Those huge green eyes were looking everywhere but at him, and her long hands were clutching that glass so tightly he half expected it to shatter. 'Ms' Morrell obviously wasn't as confident as she would have him believe.

'There is a lot of obstetrics here, but don't worry about that for now. I'll hold your hand, so to speak, for the first few weeks, and if I'm not around for some reason you can always call on Iris Sawyer. She used to be the practice nurse up until a couple of years ago. Iris is retired now, and happily so, but she doesn't mind missing a game of bowls to help out now and then, and her experience with the locals is invaluable.'

Olivia nodded, reassured by the confidence in his voice.

'Your résumé is rather impressive. I see you worked under Tony Dean in your last job. He gave you a glowing reference. I know him well. We're old friends.'

'You are?' Just the fact that this huge, daunting man was a friend of her beloved Mr Dean, the senior consultant in her former casualty department, made him somehow seem much less intimidating.

'Yes. Tony Dean was a junior consultant in Sydney when I was a mere intern. Later, our paths crossed again when I went back as a paediatric registrar. That would be five or six years ago. He moved on to Melbourne and I came here, but we still keep in touch. He's an amazing man as well as a fine doctor, but you don't need me to tell you that. Many times I've rung him for advice about a patient, or had them flown there by the air ambulance. I've probably spoken to you on the phone at some time.'

He smiled. It was a nice smile, genuine. Olivia managed to sneak a proper look. Judging by his qualifications, he'd have to be at least in his mid-thirties, but he appeared younger. He was undeniably handsome in a rugged sort of way. Unruly dark curls framed a tanned face with just a smattering of freckles over the bridge of his nose. She had been right first time—he really did look like an overgrown medical student.

'How long did you work there? I know it's in your résumé, but I can't remember offhand.'

'Five years, three as Unit Manager. I'd just left all my family behind in England, so I was feeling horribly homesick and foreign.'

'Had you been to Australia before?'

Olivia nodded. 'Yes but just on a working holiday, which is when I met my...' Olivia hesitated. 'My ex-fiancé. He was an intern then. Anyway,' Olivia added hastily, because the last thing she wanted to talk about was Jeremy, 'Mr Dean started within a couple of weeks of me. We were the ''new kids on the block'' together.'

'Why did you leave?' His question was direct and he watched as her shoulders stiffened, her hands yet again tightening convulsively around the glass.

'Personal reasons,' she answered stiffly.

Thankfully, he thought better than to push it—there

would be time for that later. Instead, he explained her new position.

'A contrast to Casualty, but there are a lot of similarities. As well as the usual coughs, colds and blood pressures, we're up against whatever they present themselves with at any hour of the day or night. From heart attacks to major farming accidents, we're the front line. You need to keep your wits about you. They breed them tough out here and they don't like a fuss. It takes a lot of skill to read between the lines. What may appear quite trivial can often be far more serious. Most tend to play down their symptoms.' He noticed her suppress a yawn.

'I'm not boring you, I hope?' he asked sharply.

Olivia sat upright, taken back by the first glimpse of him being anything other than friendly. 'Of course not.'

Clem stood up, and Olivia reluctantly admired his athletic build. 'You must be tired. You've had a long journey and it's almost midnight. I seem to think everyone else keeps my ridiculous hours. I'll let you get some sleep and I'll see you in the morning, Livvy.'

'It's Olivia, not Livvy,' she corrected him, following him to the door. 'And thank you for coming over, Dr Clemson. I'm looking forward to getting started.'

'Good. Hopefully you'll enjoy working here. And it's Clem, remember?'

Olivia suddenly felt embarrassed at how prudish she must have sounded, but she hated her name being shortened.

She watched him depart in long deliberate strides.

'Watch out for Betty and Ruby. Don't believe a word they say about me,' he shouted jokingly over his shoulder as he disappeared into the night.

As Olivia closed the door and firmly locked it, Clem rolled his eyes heavenwards. She wouldn't last five minutes. She was obviously well qualified and extremely intelligent, but she was as jumpy as a cat, and he somehow couldn't imagine her on a search and rescue. Sure, she looked stunning, he thought reluctantly then checked himself. She was probably anorexic—you didn't get a figure like that on three good meals a day.

CHAPTER TWO

OLIVIA awoke an hour before her alarm, determined to get the day off to a good start. Dougie had been right—the house was freezing. Reluctant to light a fire, instead she pulled on a pair of socks and a large jumper over her skimpy silk nightie and turned on the tiny fan heater. Jeremy would have had a heart attack if he could have seen her. Not sure how or where she'd get lunch, Olivia took advantage of the well-stocked fridge and prepared an enormous breakfast of bacon, eggs and wild mushrooms.

Mopping up the creamy yolk with a third slice of toast, she tried to decide what to wear for her first day. The usual white uniform seemed so formal, and according to the forecast it was going to be too hot for trousers. Settling on a pair of navy culottes, teamed with a white blouse and navy jacket, Olivia finally felt happy with her selection—smart but casual. She was nervous. What if the patients hated her?

With shaking hands, somehow she managed to put on her make-up, carefully trying to create a natural look. It had been a standing joke between herself and Jessica, the effort Olivia took over her appearance.

'Honestly, Olivia, you look smarter coming off duty than I do going on,' she'd often joked and Olivia would laugh back.

But her appearance was important to her. It had mattered so much to Jeremy that eventually it had rubbed off. Somehow she felt so much more confident with her 'face' on. After smoothing the wild mass of Titian ringlets into a chic French roll, she was finally satisfied.

'G'day. It's only me, Ruby.'

20

Olivia walked into the hall and watched as a huge woman burst through the front door. She had a mass of keys in her hand, as well as an array of brushes, a bucket and mop.

'Here let me help you with that,' Olivia offered.

'I'm right.' Ruby deposited her burdens on the hall floor. 'So you're Livvy? Dougie said you were a beaut, he wasn't wrong. I'll fix us a nice cup of tea before I get started. Youse must be feeling a touch nervous but, no worries, I'll take youse over and introduce you to everyone.'

Ruby was truly amazing to watch. Without even pausing for breath, she had taken Olivia's arm and seated her at the kitchen table then proceeded to fill the kettle.

'How are you finding it—a bit bewildering?'

'Just a bit,' Olivia conceded.

'Oh, we're a strange lot, that's for sure. The other nurses took one look and ran. Didn't even see the week out.' She eyed Olivia carefully.

'Well, I'm here for a lot longer than that, I can assure you,' Olivia responded with more conviction than she felt.

'Yep, I reckon you are. But a word of advice from an old chook who's been around the yard a while.' She leant over the kitchen bench and, despite the fact there was only the two of them, spoke in a theatrical whisper. 'Don't go letting the doctor upset you. Clem's bark is far worse than his bite.'

Although curious, Olivia felt she really shouldn't be discussing her employer.

'He seems very nice,' she answered noncommittally, though she secretly hoped Ruby would elaborate. Olivia didn't have to wait long!

'Oh he's golden. He snaps and snarls now and then but I just picture him as a spotty young teenager. I don't tell him that, mind, I just say ''Yes, Clem, no, Clem,'' and wait for his mood to pass—it soon does.'

'Everyone has their off days.'

'Of course, but he's got worse. It's to be expected, mind, with all he's been through. He's far too busy, and now with this new hospital and everything. I just don't know how he does it. He's always had a temper, but since Kathy passed on…' She blew her nose loudly on a hanky she'd fished from somewhere in her very ample bosom. 'Tragic, there's no other word for it.'

Olivia looked on, fascinated. This woman never stopped talking though she was busy all the while. The breakfast dishes were now washed and back in their various cupboards and the bench had been wiped down.

'It must be difficult for him,' Olivia agreed. 'He's very young to be a widower.'

'Whoever said only the good die young wasn't wrong. A real living angel was Kathy. And he's not coping. I don't care how many times he tells me he's all right—I know he's not.'

Olivia tried to steer the conversation. It really was getting too personal. 'I hear it's very busy at the surgery.'

'Tragic,' Ruby muttered, then, blowing her nose again, she stuffed the hanky back into her cleavage. 'Oh, the surgery's busy all right. Far too much work for the one doctor. It will be great when we get the hospital. A lot of the locals are opposed to it but they'll soon come round. They're just scared of change, and they'll be wary of you, too,' she added, 'with that English accent and your city ways. But youse'll soon win them over.'

'I hope so,' Olivia answered glumly.

'Of course you will,' Ruby reassured her. 'Now, come on, sweetie, we can't be here gossiping all day. You don't want to go making a bad impression.'

Walking over to the surgery, Ruby linked her arm through Olivia's. Really, Ruby was getting more maternal by the minute. Of course, just to add to Olivia's nerves, the waiting room was full. As they entered the chattering stopped and Olivia felt every face turn to her. Smiling tentatively, painfully aware of a deep blush spreading over her cheeks, she wanted to turn and run. Sitting at the desk was a middle-aged, harassed-looking woman with frizzy grey hair that had never seen conditioner.

'Thank goodness you're here,' she said as a welcome. 'I'll just let the doctor know.'

'Now, just settle a minute, Betty.' Ruby blocked her desk. 'There's always time for an introduction. This is Sister Olivia Morrell and, Sister, this is Betty. She's the receptionist here and chief cook and bottle-washer.'

'Isn't that a fact?' muttered Betty. 'I'm sorry, Sister. It's lovely to meet you, and not a moment too soon—the place is fit to burst as usual. Clem's needed over at the Hudsons. Apparently the old boy had another turn,' she added in low tones to a very attentive Ruby.

Olivia was sure that Betty shouldn't be discussing the patients with the housekeeper, but she was obviously in for a few surprises. The bush telegraph would appear somewhat similar to the hospital grapevine, and that took some beating. Even the switchboard staff had apparently known about Jeremy and Lydia.

'Anyway,' said Betty with a smile, 'we'll get there.' She nodded as a young woman came out of what appeared to be the consulting room. 'I'll take you through to Clem.'

As Olivia walked in, she noticed how much smarter Clem looked than on their first meeting. He was wearing beige trousers and a navy sports jacket, and a tie was sitting awkwardly on his thick neck. His black curls were smoother and she caught a whiff of cologne as he stood up and once again shook her hand warmly.

'Good morning, Livvy. It's good to have you on board.'

Olivia winced but Clem didn't notice.

'I did want to take some time to show you around but, as you can see from the waiting room, we're pretty full on.'

'That's all right, I'll manage,' she replied in what she hoped was an enthusiastic voice.

'Good girl.'

Olivia winced again as he nodded appreciatively. She didn't have to be a genius to see that Clem wasn't particularly politically correct.

'I'm sorry to throw you in at the deep end but I see from your résumé that you can suture, which is an absolute luxury for me. I've never had a nurse here that can stitch and, frankly, I've never had the time to teach them.'

'As long as the wound is examined by you before and after I suture, that's fine.'

Clem nodded dismissively. 'Well, in the treatment room I've got Alex Taylor. He's gashed his hand on some barbed wire while mending a fence. I've had a look and there doesn't appear to be any nerve or tendon damage, but the wound in itself is quite jagged and dirty and will need a lot of cleaning and debriding. If you could get started on him, that would be a great help. Buzz me when you're finished or if you've any concerns.'

'Right…' Olivia hesitated. 'I'll get started, then.'

'Good. He also needs a tetanus shot,' Clem added, more as an afterthought, then, picking up his fountain pen, started to write on a patient's file in a huge, untidy scrawl. Olivia stood there, not sure where to go. He hadn't exactly given her a guided tour of the place.

'Was there anything else?' he asked, without bothering to look up.

'Er, no,' she replied hesitantly. He obviously wasn't going to hold her hand. Perhaps Betty could show her where the treatment room and the equipment was. But back in the waiting room Betty was looking even more harassed than before. The phone was ringing incessantly, while she tried to force an uncooperative piece of paper into the fax machine. Oh, well, she'd just have to find her own way.

Alex was infinitely patient.

'No worries, Sister,' he said, adding reassuringly a little later, 'Take your time, Sister, I'm in no hurry.'

Olivia bustled about, trying to find suture packs and local anaesthetic. Finally, with her trolley laid out and her hands scrubbed, she was ready to start.

'Right, Alex, I'm with you now.'

'Right you are, Sister.' The elderly man nodded.

Olivia examined the wound carefully. Clem was right. It was indeed a nasty cut, very deep with untidy jagged edges and very dirty. After waiting for the local anaesthetic she had injected to take effect, Olivia once again inspected the wound, this time more thoroughly. The tendon and its sheath were visible, but thankfully intact.

'Alex, everything looks all right in there. I'm just going to give it a good clean and then I'll stitch it up. You shouldn't feel any pain, but if it does start to hurt you be sure and tell me.'

'Very good, Sister.'

Olivia was quite sure he wouldn't. Alex hadn't even let out a murmur while she'd injected the anaesthetic. 'Dr Clemson said you were repairing a fence?'

'Yep. The sheep were getting out and wandering off. I was gonna wait for me grandson to fix it, but he's away at uni till the holidays and I can't be doing chasing the stupid things. I'm too old for that.' He went on to tell Olivia about his farm and how his grandson was studying agriculture. She encouraged the conversation to take Alex's mind off his hand. Anyway, it was interesting to hear what he had to say.

'He's forever coming back from uni, full of new ideas and notions about what he wants to do with the land.'

'And does that worry you?'

''Struth, no,' Alex answered firmly. 'I'm all for progress. Mind, I'm too set in me ways to be changing things myself. But as for the young fella, he can do what he likes as far as I'm concerned. Farming's big business now it's a science.' He laughed. 'It'll all be his one day and I'm just glad he wants it. Not many young folk stay now. You just look at Clem. He wanted to stay in the city and carry on his work with the children.'

'But he came back,' Olivia ventured, curious despite herself at the insight into her boss. She had finished cleaning the hand and debriding the dead tissue. Aligning the edges, she started to suture.

'Old Dr Clemson—Clem's father—went to pieces after his wife died. His health started to fail. Clem came back to help out. He's a good sort, not like his brother Joshua—he didn't even make it in time for his own mother's funeral. Anyway, then the old fella died, God rest him. By then, though, young Clem had fallen in love with Kathy, and she would never have considered leaving here. She loved Kirrijong and it loved her.' Alex winced slightly and Olivia wasn't sure whether it was from pain or emotion.

'Is that sore, Alex? The anaesthetic is starting to wear off, but I'm just about finished now.'

'I'm all right,' he said, then continued his tale. 'Kathy belonged here, and for a while so did Clem.'

'What do you mean?'

'Well, he's busy with building the hospital and he's flat out here, but I don't reckon his heart's in it. I know he's grieving and I reckon the place has just got too many painful memories for him. I reckon we'll be lucky if he stays.'

Olivia's eyes suddenly misted over. Poor Clem. She knew all about painful memories and being alone. But if Jeremy had died? To totally lose someone… She wondered how Clem even managed to get up in the morning. At that moment she heard Clem walk into the room. He stood over her as she tied the last knot, surveying her work. The bitter tang of his cologne was a heady contrast to the chlorhexidine solution she was using on Alex's wound. Acutely aware of his closeness, her hand trembled slightly as she snipped the silk thread. Clem let out a low whistle and shook his head.

'You've made a rod for your own back Livvy. I couldn't have done a better job myself. You'll be doing all the suturing now. Right you are, then, Alex. Keep it clean and dry, and I'll see you again in a week. Here's a script for some antibiotics—that's a nasty cut and we don't want it getting infected. Any problems in the meantime and you're to come straight back.'

Alex rolled up his sleeve as Olivia approached with his tetanus shot. 'Right you are, Clem.' He got up from the trolley and added, 'I hope you don't go scaring this one off—she's a diamond.'

Olivia blushed but Clem laughed.

'I'll try not to.' He shook Alex's good hand and reminded him once again to return if needed.

'Bye, then, Sister. Thanks very much.'

'No, thank *you* Alex, for being so patient.' She smiled warmly at him and hoped all her patients would be as pleasant.

The rest of the morning passed in a whirl of dressings, recording ECGs and taking blood. An old lady eyed Olivia dubiously as she sat her down and produced a tourniquet.

'Clem normally takes my blood. I've got very difficult veins, you know.'

Taking a deep breath, Olivia forced a smile and assured the woman she knew what she was doing, adding, 'Dr Clemson is so busy this morning he didn't want to keep you sitting around, waiting for him, when you've probably got far better things to do.'

This seemed to appease her and grudgingly the woman offered her arm. Thankfully the needle went straight in.

Finally the last of the patients had been dealt with. Despite this, Betty still had to shepherd out a group of ladies from the waiting room who were conducting an impromptu mothers' meeting. Firmly closing the door, Betty let out an exaggerated sigh. 'They'll be wanting me to serve them tea and biscuits next. Come on, Sister, it's time for lunch.'

Leading Olivia through the surgery to the private part of the house she took her into the lounge room. Again, it was beautifully furnished, the walls lined with books, heavy drapes blocking out the harsh midday sun. Kathy must have used her talents in here as well. In one of the huge jade leather chairs, which clashed ravishingly with the dark crimson rug, sat a fat ginger cat. In the other chair, looking equally relaxed, sat Clem. His tie loosened, he was working his way through a large pile of sandwiches.

'Come in, come in. Ruby's done us proud as always— help yourself,' he said, offering her a plate. 'Don't wait to be asked or there won't be anything left. Isn't that right, Betty?'

Always conscious of eating in front of strangers and still full from her large breakfast, Olivia picked gingerly at a huge roast beef sandwich Betty had cheerfully put on her plate.

'Coffee, Sister?'

'Thank you, Betty, and, please, it's Olivia, remember.'

'Cream and sugar, Sister?' she asked, completely ignoring her request.

Didn't anybody here use the right name?

'No, just black will be fine.'

Clem raised his eyebrows. 'I'd suggest you tuck in, Livvy, we've got a busy afternoon ahead of us. I don't know what time we'll finish.'

'But I had a huge breakfast,' Olivia protested, then, seeing the expression on their faces, she hastily took a bite.

A talk show was on television, wives confronting their husbands' mistresses. That was all she needed.

Betty was lecturing her on the benefits of thermal underwear for night calls. 'It can be cold at night if you have to go out in a hurry,' she said, looking disapprovingly at Olivia's skinny legs. A psychologist on the television show was banging on about how wives often let themselves go after they got married. Jeremy had certainly accused her of that and they hadn't even made it up the aisle!

'I'm quite sure Olivia wouldn't be seen dead in thermals. Isn't that right?' Clem teased.

Olivia thought glumly of the small fortune she had spent on sexy underwear in an attempt to resuscitate her and Jeremy's dying sex life. All to no avail. 'Dr Clemson— Clem,' Olivia said curtly, 'as friendly as you've all been, I'm sure you wouldn't expect me to discuss my underwear—or was there something in my job description I didn't read?'

Betty coughed nervously; the television blared out the merits of keeping an air of mystery in the bedroom. Clem merely threw his head back and laughed loudly.

'Good for you. We're far too familiar here. Come on, we've got work to do.' And picking up the half-eaten sandwich left on her plate, he took a huge bite. Olivia watched distastefully and stood up.

'And if I'm not being too personal,' Clem said with more than a hint of sarcasm, 'may I suggest you go and put on some sunscreen and a hat? Half my house calls seem to be done in the middle of a field. Some insect repellent might be useful, too.'

Outside, he handed her the keys to a large black four-wheel-drive.

'This is yours, but I'll drive today, give you a chance to

get your bearings. Just put the petrol on my account at the garage.'

'Wonderful.' That was a relief. She had been beginning to wonder if 'transport provided' might mean a bus pass.

'Before we head off I'll just show you the set-up.' He opened the back door. 'As you can see, I've got all the back seats down. It's better to keep it like that so if the need arises you can transfer someone supine. There's a camp-bed mattress rolled up in the corner there, with a pillow and some blankets.' He opened up a large medical emergency box. 'I'll run through the box. Pay attention— you don't know when you might need it.'

Olivia bristled. She was only too aware of the importance of the equipment Clem was showing her—he hardly needed to tell her to listen.

'All the usual emergency drugs and intravenous solutions, all clearly labelled—giving sets, needles, syringes.' He took out each piece of equipment in turn, gave her a short lecture on its use and then replaced it. Olivia stood there, silently fuming. While she appreciated him showing her the contents, he was talking to her as if she were a first-year nursing student. 'An intubation kit,' Clem stated as he held up a plastic box clearly marked INTUBATION KIT.

'Is it?'

Clem chose to ignore her, instead painstakingly going through the various tube sizes and the appropriate ages they would be used on. Olivia automatically picked up the laryngoscope and checked that the bulb was working—it would be no fun attempting to put an intubation tube down an unconscious patient's throat if the light didn't work.

'There's spare bulbs here, but check it weekly. Have you ever intubated a patient before?' Clem enquired.

'Yes, several, but only in a controlled setting. Mr Dean insisted his senior nursing staff knew how, just in case. Anyway, it helps assisting doctors if you've done it yourself.' She thought for a moment. 'But I've never intubated anyone without supervision.' Clem heard the note of tension creep into her voice.

'And hopefully you won't have to. You can always bag them until help arrives, but who knows what can happen? At least you know your way around the kit. You can have a go, that's got to be better than doing nothing and watching someone die.' Olivia nodded glumly, not for the first time wondering just what she had taken on.

'Now the defibrillator. It's pretty standard, you can run a three-channel ECG off this model—'

'I've used that type before,' Olivia interrupted.

'Here's the on-off switch,' Clem continued, blatantly ignoring her again. 'Keep it plugged in overnight to charge it, but just run the cord through the Jeep window into the garage wall. Are you listening? I hope you're taking all this in,' he snapped rudely.

'I've used a defibrillator before—this model, in fact. I know what I'm doing.'

'I'm sure you do,' he said through gritted teeth, 'but when I ring you at one in the morning to come and assist me in an emergency, I need to be sure you know exactly where all the equipment is and how it works. It's no good you driving off in a hurry and leaving the bloody defibrillator still charging on the garage floor.'

'Obviously not,' Olivia retorted. She was nervous enough about her new responsibilities, without him treating her like the village idiot. 'I'm grateful to you for showing me things, but I really don't need a total re-train. If I don't know or understand something then I'll ask.' She stood there resolutely, staring defiantly into his angry, haughty face, awaiting his wrath, but it never came.

'Well, just make sure you do,' he said after what seemed an age. Turning his large back on her, he deftly replaced the equipment.

With her face burning, Olivia made her way to the passenger seat. She knew she had been right to stand up to him. He had to treat her, if not as an equal, at least with some respect.

Climbing into the driver's seat, he started the ignition. 'We'll go the back way. It's a short cut but don't use it till you're comfortable with the Jeep.' And without looking over once, he gave her a run-down on their first patient. 'The first port of call is the Jean Hunt, for her postnatal check. She's just had her fourth baby. A son after three daughters...young Sam. He's six weeks old now.' Clem skilfully guided the car around the tight bends.

'Oh, yes,' Olivia recalled. 'Dougie mentioned them. They must be thrilled.'

'Not exactly,' Clem replied grimly. 'Everyone's thrilled except Mum.'

'Oh, dear.'

Clem finally glanced over at her, realising she understood the situation.

'Exactly.'

Olivia remembered only too well the tearful mums on the maternity ward, trying desperately to appear happy to relatives and wondering why on earth they'd been feeling so miserable and unable to cope.

Clem continued, 'After an extremely long and exhausting labour with a difficult posterior presentation, young Master Hunt entered the world quite healthy, screaming his head off, and he hasn't stopped since. A complete contrast to the girls, who were the most placid little sheilas you could imagine. Alicia, the youngest, actually had to be woken for her feeds for the first couple of months. Not only does Jean have a husband and three other children to cope with, she's also dealing with a never-ending stream of well-wishers bringing little blue gifts and telling her how delighted she must be feeling.'

'Poor thing,' Olivia sympathised. 'How's his weight?'

'Borderline. He's gaining, but not as much as I'd like.'

Olivia thought for a moment.

'Could he have reflux?' she suggested.

Clem shrugged. 'I really don't think so, though I have considered it. I've seen a lot of reflux babies but Sam just doesn't quite fit the picture. I think it's more Jean.'

'Is she breastfeeding?'

'Trying to, but I'm going to suggest she puts him on the bottle today.'

Olivia couldn't believe what she was hearing. How behind was this place? Everyone knew you encouraged breastfeeding.

He looked over again. 'What's wrong, you don't approve?' Clem parked the car and turned around to face her.

She looked at him properly for the first time, and realised just how attractive he really was. 'It's not a question of whether I approve or not. I was taught to promote breastfeeding, that's all. To give in after such a short time seems strange to me.'

'Look, I do see your point. Breast is best and all that, but only if it's working. When it isn't, the bottle is fantastic.'

Olivia opened her mouth to argue but he cut her short.

'There's no breastfeeding mothers' support group here, no lactation consultant to call in, just the help you and I can offer. You may have only done a morning here, but you can surely see how stretched we are.' He held up his hand to silence her as she again attempted to put her point. 'Let me finish, then you can have your say.'

Olivia snapped her mouth closed and folded her arms.

'I've been round nearly every day since Sam was born, but there's not much more I can do. He's healthy, he's just hungry. For whatever reason, breastfeeding just isn't working this time. Anyway, Jean's far more experienced than you or I—after all, she's successfully fed three children. It's a bit like taking snow to the Eskimos, offering her advice on her feeding technique.'

Olivia grudgingly nodded.

'And as chauvinistic as it may sound to a liberated young woman like yourself, Mr Hunt will be back from a hard day's work at the farm this evening. He'll want to come back to a tidy house and a meal. It doesn't mean he loves her any less than the sensitive twenty-first century men you may mix with, it's just the way it is here. And I can tell you now that Jean isn't going to take a stand for sisterhood and to heck with routine.'

Olivia digested his speech. She actually understood far more than he realised. She herself had desperately wanted to start a family as soon as they'd got married. But as with their elusive wedding date, Jeremy had wanted to wait, for what she hadn't been quite sure. The thought of Jeremy coming home to a messy house, a crying baby and a hysterical mother made her realise he wasn't the modern, liberated man he liked to think he was. Taking her silence as dissent Clem went further.

'I could prescribe anti-depressants or tell her to hang in there till things improve, but I'm not prepared to do that, at least not this early in the piece. That's not the kind of medicine I practise.'

And despite the fact she had indeed only worked a morning with him, Olivia knew that already. It was obvious from the adoration of his patients that he was a wonderful caring doctor. Still, she wasn't prepared to give in that easily. 'I still think you should go in there with an open mind,' she said defiantly, but, watching his face darken, wished she'd held her tongue. She probably wouldn't last the week out, like her predecessors.

'May I suggest something?' Clem said slowly.

'Of course.' Olivia nodded weakly. Perhaps he was going to tell her to remember her place.

'Maybe it should be *you* that goes in to the house with an open mind. In fact, why don't you decide what Jean should do?' he suggested.

'And if I don't come down on your side, you'll simply override me,' she retorted.

Clem shook his head. 'You don't know me very well. Of course, I could override you but I won't. It's your call.' He picked up his doctor's bag, effectively ending the conversation, and got out of the vehicle. Striding to the front door, Olivia had to half run to keep up with him. Knocking firmly, he turned. 'Remember, an open mind.'

Jean Hunt opened the door still in her dressing-gown, her hair unbrushed, her eyes red and swollen from crying.

'Oh, Clem, I'm so glad you're here. He's been screaming all morning.' She ushered them through to the family room, apologising for the mess. The house was in chaos. Toys littered the floor and piles of washing lay over the chairs and sofa. The morning's breakfast dishes were still on the breakfast bar. 'Please, sit down,' she said to Olivia, removing a pile of nappies.

Clem peered into the crib. 'He's asleep now.'

'Yes, but it won't last.' Her eyes brimmed. 'Can I get you a cup of tea?'

Clem turned to Olivia. Taking her cue, she jumped up.

'I'll sort out the tea. Why don't you let Clem examine you while Sam is asleep?'

Clem nodded appreciatively.

'He'll be awake before you know it. Six weeks old and he's hardly slept for more than two hours at a time. The girls were so easy—I just don't know what it is I'm doing wrong. Brian's so thrilled at having a boy, he just doesn't understand...' Jean's voice broke and her shoulders shook with emotion.

Clem, towering over her, put his arms around her heaving shoulders and spoke softly. 'Come on, Jean. Let's go through to the bedroom and I'll do your postnatal check, then we'll sit down over a nice cuppa and try to sort something out.' Gently he led her away.

After switching on the kettle, Olivia hastily did the breakfast dishes and wiped down the benches. The family room wasn't dirty, just untidy. She put the toys back into their box and started to sort out the laundry, folding the nappies into a neat pile and placing the rest into the groaning ironing basket. The place looked a lot better, and by the time Clem retuned she had made the tea.

'Jean's just getting dressed.' He raised his eyebrows 'You've been busy.'

Jean was eternally grateful. 'Sister, you didn't have to do that.'

'No problem, Jean. I'm glad to help.'

While they drank their tea, Jean, in a faltering voice, told them her problems. 'If I could just get a decent sleep and the house in order I'd be all right, but Sam takes for ever to feed. Then, when I finally get him off, no sooner have I put him down than he's awake and screaming again. I'm at my wits end.' She ran her fingers through her unwashed hair.

'Does Sam have any long sleeps at all?' Clem asked.

'Sometimes, at about five, which is useless for me. The girls are home from school then, wanting their tea, and then Brian gets in. As the girls go off to bed up gets the little fella, and that's me for the rest of the night, trying to keep him quiet so that Brian can get a good sleep.'

'Could Brian get up to him for a couple of nights, at the weekend perhaps so you could get a break?' Olivia volunteered. 'Perhaps if you expressed some milk?'

Jean shook her head. 'He's up at five a.m. to go to the

farm. It's the same at weekends—the cows still need milking. I can't expect him to be awake at night with the kids.'

Olivia finally realised the woman's predicament. Just then Sam stirred and let out a piercing cry, which made them all jump. It was amazing just how much noise a small baby could make. Clem picked up the infant as Jean started to weep.

'What's wrong with him, Clem?'

'Put him to your breast, Jean, and let me see you feed him.' Olivia spoke calmly, and Clem handed Sam to his mother. The irate baby arched his back and butted against Jean's breast, searching frantically for and finding her nipple. He latched on and mercifully relaxed. Making little whimpering noises, he suckled hungrily.

'Very good, Jean, you're doing wonderfully,' Clem encouraged. 'Just try and relax.' At that point Sam let out a furious wail and the angry protest started again.

Jean was just about at breaking point. 'What's wrong with him?' she screamed above the ear-splitting shrieks of her son.

Olivia walked over and gently took the baby from the distraught woman. The baby snuffled against her. Olivia felt his hot, angry little face against hers, breathing in the familiar baby smell. Rocking Sam, gently trying to soothe him, she contemplated Jean's situation. For all her knowledge and training she had no real experience. Here was a woman who had borne four babies to her nil. She had a husband and children to care for and a house she was proud of. The well-rehearsed platitudes of 'persevere' and 'things will get better' seemed woefully inadequate. Olivia could see what was wrong. Jean had plenty of milk but she wasn't letting down, probably because she was too tense. Appearances mattered, and to tell this woman to ignore the housework and concentrate on the baby, to get a take-away and not worry about dinner, would be like speaking a foreign language. Heck, there wasn't a burger bar for two hundred kilometres.

Clem watched Olivia closely as she rocked the baby. Sam rooted hopefully and, finding her finger, sucked hungrily, but again there came the same wail of frustration.

'He's hungry, Jean,' Olivia said.

'He can't be. I fed him just an hour ago. You saw me just try—that's not what he wants.'

Olivia gently but firmly explained about the letdown reflex. 'It's automatic in some women, as it was for you with the girls. But anxiety, tension, lack of sleep—any one of these can affect it. It's a vicious circle. The more Sam cries, the harder it is for you to relax and for your milk to get through. Have you considered trying him with some formula?'

'But breast milk's best—everyone says so,' Jean protested.

'A contented mum and baby are what's important. Anyway, giving him a bottle now doesn't automatically mean you have to give up on breastfeeding. Perhaps after a couple of feeds and a good sleep you'll be ready to do battle again. You could maybe give him a bottle at night and concentrate on breastfeeding in the day. There are lots of options. Even if he does end up on the bottle, you've given Sam your colostrum in the first few days, which is full of antibodies, and he's had six weeks on the breast. You've done very well.'

'What do you think?' Jean turned to Clem.

'I totally agree with Livvy.' He stood up. 'I've got some formula samples in the car. Why don't you make him up a bottle and we'll see how he goes?'

Half an hour later a much happier Jean cuddled her satisfied son. Young Master Sam made contented little noises.

'Feeling better now?' Clem enquired.

'Much, but I'm a bit disappointed.'

'Well, don't be,' Olivia said firmly. 'Like I said, it might be a different ball game tomorrow. But whatever you do, don't go getting stressed—just enjoy each other.'

'Thanks ever so.' She looked over at Olivia. 'You've both been wonderful.'

'We haven't finished yet.' Clem darted outside and returned with a huge casserole pot. 'Ruby's forever trying to fatten me up. There's more than enough here to feed the family, Jean.' He took Sam from her and put him gently into the crib. 'Now, the place is tidier, the baby's asleep and dinner's taken care off. You get to bed.'

'I should get some ironing done,' Jean protested, but Olivia quickly jumped in.

'Don't you dare.' She shooed her down the hall.

'I wouldn't argue with Sister Morrell if I were you, Jean. I've a feeling she'd win. Now, off to bed, Doctor's orders. We'll see ourselves out.'

Back in the car Clem praised her. 'You did a great job in there.'

'Only because I listened to you first,' Olivia admitted. 'I shudder to think of the mess I'd have made if you hadn't forewarned me.'

'I think you're being a bit hard on yourself,' he said kindly. 'We'll need to keep a close eye on Jean, make sure things are improving—she's on a short fuse at the moment. Let me know if you're worried about her.' He turned and smiled. 'It's good having you on board, Livvy.'

As she opened her mouth to correct him he started the engine. Oh, what was the point? She might just as well get used to it.

The rest of the afternoon passed quickly. In each home they were made welcome. Despite Clem's sometimes brutal honesty and arrogant assumptions, it was obvious the patients all adored him. Everywhere they went the patients insisted on making a cup of tea. As if he hadn't had a drink all day, Clem gratefully accepted and listened as they chatted. Finally, armed with a bag of lemons and some lamingtons, they had finished the rounds.

'For a day's work well done, I'll buy you dinner. It's time for you to visit the local hotel.'

'But we can't. I'm in my work clothes,' Olivia wailed. The thought of having to talk to him socially terrified her.

'I'm not intending to get you drunk, I can assure you, but it's nearly seven already and I'm sure you're about as keen to cook dinner as I am.'

Driving into the main street, he parked and escorted her straight into a bistro. Gorgeous smells wafted from the kitchen and Olivia realised how hungry she really was. Again Clem was greeted like a long-lost friend.

'G'day there. The usual, Clem? And what about the young lady?'

'An orange juice, please.'

Clem remembered his manners and introduced her. 'This is Olivia Morrell, the new sister at the practice.'

'Pleased to meet you, Livvy,' the landlord greeted her cheerfully. Casually holding her elbow, Clem led her over to a table by the window and went back to the bar to fetch their drinks. Olivia gazed out of the window at the miles of land stretched out before her. The road continued far into the horizon. It was magnificent. She wished she were here with Jeremy. It had been so long since they'd been away together or even out for a meal, just the two of them. There had always been work, or a function to attend. Perhaps if she'd insisted, or just gone ahead and booked a weekend away, maybe they could somehow have prevented the mess they were in.

'Daydreaming?'

Olivia jumped as Clem placed their drinks on the table. 'I was just admiring the view.'

'Yes it's pretty spectacular,' he agreed. 'As are the pies

here. I took the liberty of ordering for you. They do the best steak pie I've ever tasted.'

'Sounds marvellous.'

Conversation was surprisingly easy. He was very good company, with a wicked, cynical sense of humour. Olivia felt herself start to relax as he told her tales of the locals. The pie, as promised, was spectacular, the sauce rich and spicy. Mopping her plate with a second bread roll, she felt Clem staring at her.

'What?' she said, hastily putting down her roll.

'Nothing. I'm just glad you're enjoying the food,' he remarked.

'And why shouldn't I be? It's delicious.'

Clem surprised himself at how much pleasure he took in watching her unwind. For the first time since they'd met she was actually looking at him for more than ten seconds when he spoke. The constant fiddling with her earrings or hair had stopped. He decided to broach a question he had been wondering about. 'You said last night your "ex-fiancé". Was the break-up very recent?' Those stunning green eyes frantically looked over to the bar as if in a silent plea for help, her hand immediately shooting up to her earrings.

'Yes.' Olivia replied reluctantly.

'Were you engaged for long?'

'We were together five years, engaged for two.'

Clem let out a low whistle. 'Ouch,' he said simply, and took a drink of his beer. For a second she thought the conversation was over but he wasn't letting her off so easily.

'He's not exactly a fast mover. Why weren't you married?' he probed.

Olivia sighed, wishing he would just drop it. 'We were happy the way we were, there wasn't any need to rush,' she stated, bringing out the old platitudes she had used on her friends and parents so many times in the past.

'Rubbish,' Clem said rudely. 'I have a theory about couples in long engagements and so far I've always been right.' He paused. 'Do you want to hear it?'

'Not particularly, but I've a feeling I'm going to.'

Clem grinned and continued. 'One is desperate for the commitment, the other is holding out, but both pretend a long engagement is what they want. It's the same with couples who live together—there's always one holding back. Am I right?'

He was, of course, damn him, but she certainly wasn't going to let him know as much.

'Actually, no, you're not. Jeremy's been under a lot of pressure recently. We were waiting till he made consultant. There wasn't time to concentrate on a wedding as well.'

'Well, I'd have made time,' Clem insisted. 'I'd have snapped you up years ago.'

It was an innocent statement, made entirely in the context of the conversation, but for some reason Olivia felt herself start to blush. Clem didn't seem to notice.

'So what does he think about you being out here?'

'He doesn't know.'

'You're not some fugitive on the missing persons list, are you?' The tone of his voice made her look up and she was relieved to see he was smiling.

'He's a bit too busy with his new girlfriend, I would think, to be looking for me.'

Clem took a long drink of his beer. 'So one call from Jeremy and I could lose the only decent nurse this town has seen in months.'

'I'm more responsible than that,' Olivia retorted quickly. 'I'm not just some puppy dog that can be summoned. I've accepted the job and I'm aware of my obligations.'

'Whoa.' He raised his hands.

'Anyway,' she continued, 'as I've only been here a day, aren't you judging me rather hastily?'

'On the contrary. I believe in first impressions, though I must admit I was wrong about your eating habits.'

Olivia gave him a questioning look but he didn't elaborate.

'Kathy always said I knew at a glance…' He took a hasty sip of his drink and then in a soft voice he continued, 'Kathy was my wife. She died,' he said simply. Now it was his turn to avoid her gaze.

'I heard. I'm so sorry. How long ago?'

'It will be two years in a few months, but the way it feels it might just as well have been yesterday.' He drained his glass. 'Hold onto your heart, Livvy, because you only get hurt in the end. I sometimes wonder if the pleasure of being in love is worth the pain.' He gave her a rueful smile. 'Listen to us two lonely hearts getting maudlin.' The carefree shift in his tone did nothing to disguise the sadness hanging in the air. 'Can I get you another drink?'

Olivia reached for her purse. 'No, it's my turn. I'm going to have a coffee.' Like her, he obviously didn't want to talk about his loss. The difference was, she was too polite to push it. 'Can I get you one?'

Clem shook his head.

'Another beer, then, or a cup of tea perhaps?' she offered.

'Olivia, sit down a moment. There's something I must tell you,' Clem said in a serious voice. She tentatively sat down. What on earth could it be?

'You must promise not to tell any of the patients this. If it were to get out, so many people would be offended.'

Olivia nodded nervously. Whatever was he going to say? She'd only known him five minutes.

He leant over the table, taking her hand and drawing her nearer, looking around to make sure nobody could hear. Leaning forward, she listened intently.

'I hate tea. Absolutely loathe the stuff, and every day I'm forced to drink gallons.'

'What?' Olivia looked up at him, startled. Was that it? Throwing his head back, he started to laugh, so loudly, in fact, that a few of their fellow diners turned around, smiling, to see what was so funny. Unperturbed, he carried on until finally she joined in. It had been so long since she'd truly laughed and, what's more, she marvelled, it felt wonderful.

CHAPTER THREE

SITTING at her kitchen table, Olivia attempted to pen a reply to Jessica's letter. A niggling sore throat which had been troubling her for a couple of days seemed to have come out in force. Pulling a face as she downed some soluble aspirin, Olivia reread Jessica's letter. Although apparently still full on with Lydia, Jeremy was pestering Jessica to find out where Olivia had moved to. She took some solace when she read how awful he was looking—black rings under his eyes, unironed shirts, creased suits and snapping at everyone. Which was most unlike Jeremy, who saved his mood swings for the home front. At work he was calm, unruffled and totally pleasant to one and all.

Perhaps he was actually missing her, realising what a terrible mistake he'd made. What if he did get in touch? Could she take him back after all he'd put her through? Olivia knew the answer should be no, yet a part of her couldn't let go. He had been her first real relationship, her first and only lover. The reason she had left her family and friends in England and travelled to the other side of the world. Letting go just wasn't that easy.

She had been in Kirrijong a month now. The locals were starting to accept her. Alex had returned to have his sutures removed, bringing her a bunch of proteas and several bottles of home-made tomato sauce. Her fridge and pantry groaned with the weight of home-made wines and chutneys, nectarines and lemons. They waved as she passed in her black Jeep and had started to make appointments to see her without Clem. It felt good to be liked and wanted. Yet each night she crept into the huge wooden bed and, while hating

45

herself for being so weak, longed to feel Jeremy's arms around her, ached for the warmth of human touch.

It was Wednesday and she wasn't due on duty till eleven. Normally Olivia arrived early anyway, there was always more than enough work to do, but she had allowed herself the luxury of a lie-in and the chance to catch up on some letters. She hadn't been feeling herself at all lately. Initially Olivia had assumed it had been the pressure she was under, but now, with this niggling throat and persistent headaches, she began to suspect she was coming down with the same flu that seemed to be sweeping the rest of the town. Yelping as she noticed the clock edging past ten-thirty, Olivia dressed quickly. The morning had caught up with her.

Breezing into the surgery bang on eleven, she smiled confidently at the now mostly familiar faces.

'Morning, Betty. Are these for me?' Picking up a pile of patients' files, she started to flick through them.

'Yes. One's for stitching—he's out the back. And there's an ECG that needs doing—Clem wants it done as soon as you arrive. And a word of warning—he's not in the sunniest of moods this morning.'

Olivia raised her eyebrows. So she was finally going to see the legendary dark side of the good Dr Clemson.

'He came in like a bear with a sore head this morning and then, to make matters worse, her ladyship arrived.'

'Her ladyship?' Olivia enquired, not having a clue whom Betty was talking about.

'Oh you haven't had the pleasure of meeting his lady friend, Charlotte, have you?'

'His lady friend?' Olivia recalled the first night she had arrived in Kirrijong, when Clem had failed to meet her. Funny, although she'd heard what Dougie had said, by the way Clem had spoken about Kathy she'd just assumed there was no one else. Anyway, it didn't matter to her who he went out with, of course it didn't, Olivia thought firmly. She was just surprised, that's all.

'If you can call her a lady.' Betty lowered her voice. 'What he sees in her I'll never—' She coughed suddenly and started to shuffle some papers. 'Speak of the devil.'

Clem held open his door and Olivia felt her jaw drop for there, walking out of his office and looking completely out of place in a doctor's surgery in the middle of the bush, was six feet in heels of absolute drop-dead gorgeous sophistication.

Dressed in an immaculate white suit, her skirt at mid-thigh revealing the longest bronze legs imaginable, Charlotte Ross sauntered over to the desk, tossing her raven black mane. There was arrogance about her, an air of superiority, that, Olivia guessed, came when you were that beautiful. She looked straight through Olivia and Betty and picked up the telephone, barking orders at Dougie who doubled as the local taxi. She shook a cigarette out of her packet. Olivia felt her temper rise. Surely she wasn't going to light up here? Charlotte obviously had some discretion, though, and put the cigarette back in the pack.

'Thanks, Clemmie, I'll see you this afternoon,' she purred in a voice quite different from the one she'd used on Dougie.

Clem nodded. 'Fine. I'll see you then,' he answered. Charlotte had obviously done nothing to cheer him up, judging by the murderous expression on his face.

Catching sight of Olivia still standing there, holding the patients' files, he turned to her. 'So you finally managed to get here, then?' he barked.

'I beg your pardon?'

'You're late,' Clem announced to the waiting room.

'Sister's been here a good ten minutes…' Betty soothed.

'She's getting you to make excuses for her now, is she?' he demanded of poor Betty.

Olivia couldn't believe what she was hearing. She looked around the now silent waiting room at the expectant faces. 'If I might have a word in your office, Dr Clemson,' she said in as steady voice as she could manage, given the circumstances.

'I'm too busy, and so are you. You've already kept the patients waiting quite long enough as it is. I'll deal with you later.' And disappearing into his office, he left Olivia quite literally shaking with rage.

A deep, throbbing voice with the hint of a fake American accent broke the silence. 'I'm going to wait in the lounge. Call me when my taxi arrives,' Charlotte ordered. Tossing her hair again, she waltzed out of the surgery, though not before she'd managed to smirk at Olivia.

Fuming, Olivia got through the rest of the morning. How dare he talk to her like that, let alone in front of the patients? The atmosphere progressively worsened as the day continued, with Clem barking orders and constantly buzzing her on the intercom. 'Do this. Fetch that. Where are the results for this patient?' Olivia did as she was told, for the time being. The last thing she wanted was another scene in front of the patients. It was fruitless, as well as unprofessional.

'But if he thinks he's getting away with it he's wrong. As soon as surgery is over I'll let him know exactly what I think of his behaviour.'

'You'll just make things worse. Let it pass, he'll settle down soon,' Betty pleaded.

Finally the last patient had been dealt with. Olivia made herself a cup of coffee and took a half-hearted bite of an apple. Sitting at her desk, she started to write up her notes. It seemed that no matter what you did in nursing these days it produced a never-ending pile of paperwork to be completed. A shadow over her file told her Clem was standing at the desk, but she didn't look up. She certainly wasn't going to make an apology easy for him.

'I would have thought you'd had plenty of time to eat this morning, judging by how late you were.'

Well, she evidently wasn't going to get an apology. Olivia looked up from her notes. Clem's face looked down at her, so hostile she could hardly believe the change, but she refused to be intimidated. 'I most certainly was not late this morning. I was due to start at eleven, which I did. It's now two forty-five and I'm working through my break.'

'How very noble,' he said sarcastically.

That really was the limit. So she had been warned of his black unreasonable moods. So he was up to his neck in work. So the man was a widower. If he thought she was going to scuttle into the corner and hide like Betty, he was wrong. She'd had enough of irrational mood swings from Jeremy to last her a lifetime. She certainly didn't need it from him. 'No, Dr Clemson, it isn't noble, merely necessary. The files have to be written up and I have to eat. I am human after all, although judging by the way you treated me this morning I doubt you either noticed or cared.' She watched his face darken with rage. If he'd been angry before, he was really mad now.

'And what exactly,' he said menacingly, sitting down opposite her, 'is it that you don't like about my behaviour?'

Olivia took a deep breath. Oh, well, she might as well let him have it. She obviously wasn't going to be here for much longer. 'I don't like being spoken to like a naughty child, particularly in front of the patients. If you have a problem with my work, discuss it with me in your office. I also don't like you taking your beastly temper out on me.'

'Anything else?' he snapped.

'Yes, actually, there is.' She was gaining momentum now. 'I most definitely don't appreciate being told I'm late for work, or you implying that I'm taking excessive breaks, when the truth is I'm working way over the hours you specified in my contract. I don't mind working late, every night if necessary. I don't mind coming in early. However, if I'm due to start work at eleven and I have no indication that you need me earlier, don't get angry with me for not being here. I'm not a mind-reader.' Her temper had bubbled to the surface.

'Well, that's obvious,' he replied. 'Because if you could read my mind you'd be ringing up the unions, claiming unfair dismissal. I hadn't realised you were so militant, Sister.'

Olivia stood up. She'd had enough of this ridiculous conversation. 'Are you sacking me, doctor? Because if you are just say so and I'll be straight out of here.'

Clem got up. Despite her height, he was still a good head taller than she was. Olivia stood there, her face defiant. He wasn't going to intimidate her.

'That would seem to be your standard answer to any criticism or confrontation. But where are you going to run to this time? You've exhausted Victoria and New South Wales. Perhaps you should cross the border and see how you go in Queensland—until the next time someone pulls you up, that is. Still, there's always the Northern Territory.'

He was poisonous. That was the utter limit. How dare he drag her personal life into this? How dared he make such unjust assumptions about her? Stunned by his contemptuous remarks, she stood there, her face white, literally shaking with rage. What on earth could she say to that? He opened his mouth to speak but Olivia found her voice.

'Don't.' She put her hands up in front of her. 'Don't you *ever* speak to me like that again.' And something in her voice told him he'd totally overstepped the mark.

'Livvy…'

She shook her head. Whatever he was going to say, she

didn't want to hear it. There were no excuses to justify that outburst.

'Just get on with your work. I'm going on a house call, you can page me if you need me. I don't know how long I'll be.' The contempt in his voice had gone but his arrogance remained. Refusing to look at him, she stood there quite still as he haughtily left the surgery.

Only when the door had safely slammed behind him did Olivia promptly burst into tears. Clem's dramatic exit was ruined somewhat when he had to return to retrieve his car keys. Seeing her sitting at the desk, weeping, a huge wave of guilt swept over him. To have reduced this proud, troubled woman to tears gave him no pleasure. His apology was genuine and heartfelt.

'I've made you cry. I'm sorry.'

It was Olivia's turn to be difficult. 'Don't give yourself the credit.'

'I can be so pig-headed at times. I really didn't mean it.' He handed her a tissue from the box on the desk, which she accepted with a sniff.

'I'm not crying about you. I've come up against far more arrogant doctors than you in my time.'

'I'll try to take that as a compliment.'

Olivia managed a faint smile.

'If it's not just me that's upset you, who has?' The gentleness in his voice touched her. He sat on the desk, putting a tender hand on her shoulder, troubled by how fragile she felt. 'I know I'm not your favourite person after today's episode but I'm here if you want to talk.'

Olivia felt her anger evaporate. She so badly wanted to talk, to share, and Clem did seem genuine in his interest. Perhaps a man's opinion would offer some insight.

'A friend wrote this morning. It would appear that the object of Jeremy's desire still isn't me.' Clem didn't respond and she continued tentatively, 'I took some refuge in the fact that he looks awful, hoping that perhaps he's missing me after all. But who am I kidding? It's probably all the sex that's exhausting him.'

He smiled down at her, not moving his arm. 'What's she like?'

Olivia tried to describe Lydia objectively, fighting back the image of the scarlet woman with six-inch nails and a cleavage to die for. 'Well, I'd like to call her a bimbo, but she's actually very clever. She's his intern. Jeremy's a surgical registrar,' she explained. 'She's also very...' Olivia hesitated '...pretty. All boobs and behind, blonde hair, baby blue eyes.

'I never saw it coming,' she went on. 'Lydia's the antithesis of what Jeremy usually likes. She's scatty, disorganised, but apparently she made him feel "needed".'

'Not exactly the "burn your bra" type, then?' Clem said dryly, and Olivia managed a shaky smile.

'She makes me feel like a frigid spinster, yet I was the one engaged to him.'

'You're hardly relegated to the desperate and dateless pile yet,' Clem reasoned. 'You're gorgeous.'

'Jeremy didn't seem to think so.'

'Jeremy sounds like an idiot,' he stated, but feeling her body tense under his hand he realised he was on the wrong track.

'He's just confused,' Olivia said defensively.

'Maybe, but he doesn't have the right to hurt you like this.'

'He's hurting, too.'

Clem doubted this. He had met more Jeremys in his career than he cared to remember. So pumped up by the instant adoration and authority a white coat gave them, they actually felt they deserved their affairs. It didn't matter who got hurt in the process, just as long as they got what they assumed was their right. And in this case Olivia was the victim.

Clem's face hardened and his grip involuntarily tightened on her shoulder. For Jeremy to have reduced this strong, eloquent woman to tears and self-doubt made him churn inside. He hoped Jeremy got what he deserved. Olivia wriggled away uncomfortably. 'I'm fine now. Thank you for listening.' The mask was back on, her guard up.

'Look, Olivia, I'm always here if you want to talk.'

Olivia shook her head and blew her nose loudly.

Cursing himself for his poor handling of the situation, he remained seated and tried to revive the conversation, determined to be less antagonistic. 'Why don't I come over tonight and we can talk properly?'

Olivia shook her head. 'No, but thanks, anyway. I'll be all right now.' She picked up her pen. The conversation was over. Clem hesitated, as if about to say something. Olivia's pen paused over the file, his hand moved to her face and, picking up a loose curl that had escaped, he smoothed it behind her ear. The seemingly innocent gesture caught her completely unawares.

'I'm not taking no for an answer. I'll bring dessert.'

He left the surgery, this time closing the door gently behind him. Olivia sat there, stunned. How on earth had that just happened? A few moments ago he had been the second most loathsome man to walk this earth and now she was having dinner with him. Putting her hand up to her face where he had touched her, she felt her burning cheeks, then, firmly shaking her head, she set back to work.

Finally the last of the files had been written up, and after packing her bag with various bandages, dressing packs and solutions Olivia headed into town to make her own house calls. There were only a couple of dressings that needed doing and one postnatal visit. Which should, she reasoned, leave her with plenty of time to have a long bath and prepare a nice dinner for herself and Clem.

It was a pleasant drive into town, and Olivia took her time. Approaching an old Queenslander-style home, she admired the immaculate garden with an abundance of flowers that had obviously been lovingly tended. An elderly woman on the veranda waved to her as she passed and Olivia cheerfully waved back, relishing the laid-back friendliness of this tiny slice of Australia. But the woman kept on waving and, just giving herself time to indicate, Olivia swerved the Jeep and bought it to a hasty halt. Jumping down, the hot afternoon sun's glare made it impossible to see the woman. Holding her hand up to shield her eyes, Olivia called out.

'Is everything all right?'

The elderly woman came into focus. Breathless from running, her lined face was full of concern. 'I thought you were the doctor. I saw the Jeep,' she gasped. 'I've been trying to call him. It's Harry—he's got these chest pains. I called an ambulance, he's really crook. Please, help.'

In no time Olivia helped the lady into the passenger seat and, executing a hasty U-turn, crunched the gears and sped the short distance up the drive and back to the house. The journey was all it took to glean that the lady was called Narelle and was Harry's wife. Coming to a sharp halt, Olivia was tempted to go in first and assess the situation, but she kept a cool head and instead quickly opened up the back of the Jeep, grabbing the emergency pack. Despite its considerable weight, she ran into the house.

The drapes were pulled and after the brightness of outside it took a couple of seconds till she could see in the cool dark room, but one look at the elderly man's grey, sweaty face was all she needed to know the trouble he was in. Slumped in a large armchair, he was obviously in a lot of pain. Olivia turned on the oxygen cylinder, her moist palms making it difficult to turn the lever. Gently she placed an oxygen mask over his face.

'Harry, I'm Olivia Morrell, Clem's nursing sister. Show me where the pain is.'

A shaking hand came up to the centre of his chest.

'And does it go anywhere else?' He shook his head. Realising it would be too much exertion for him to speak, she addressed Narelle as she hastily attached the cardiac monitor. 'When did the pains start?'

'About half an hour ago. He was just pottering in the garden. I told him it was too hot to be out there.'

'Has he ever had anything like this before?'

Narelle shook her head. 'Nothing. He's as strong as a mallee bull is our Harry.'

'No angina, high blood pressure, breathing problems, diabetes?' Olivia ran through a list of various medical complaints.

'Nothing. He just has a flu shot once a year.'

'How old is Harry, and is he allergic to anything you know of?'

'Sixty-eight and, no, he's not allergic to anything.'

Olivia scribbled down Clem's mobile number. 'Narelle, try Clem on this number.'

'I have been. I got it from the answering machine at the surgery but he's out of range. I left a message with his paging service. I've been trying to get hold of Betty but she's not home.'

So she really was on her own.

'It's his heart, isn't it, Sister? Oh, God, he's not going to die, is he?' Narelle started to panic, her voice rising to a crescendo, and Olivia knew she had to keep her calm. Any upset would only further distress Harry.

'Get me a small glass of water. I'm going to give Harry some aspirin.' The simple instruction was all it took to stop the woman's mounting hysteria, and she dutifully nodded.

But before Narelle even had time to turn for the kitchen the situation suddenly intensified as Harry's condition deteriorated rapidly. His eyes rolled back into his head and he slumped further into the chair. Deftly Olivia felt for his carotid pulse. Unable to palpate it, she glanced over at the monitor, which confirmed her fear—Harry had gone into cardiac arrest. Olivia gave him a hefty thump on the chest in a bid to kick-start his heart.

'Narelle, help me get him onto the floor,' she ordered, but Narelle was completely hysterical. There was no point in trying to calm her down. That would have taken time and that was what she was fighting against. Dragging him down to the floor by herself, trying to block out Narelle's desperate screams, Olivia worked quickly but methodically.

Having hastily attached the ambu-bag to the oxygen, she inserted the small curved tube that would keep Harry's airway open and enable her to give him the essential oxygen he so desperately needed. Then she rhythmically pumped his chest. Her cardiac massage was practised and effective, even managing to stop Narelle in her tracks as the regular bleeping of Harry's heart emitted from the monitor. But as soon as Olivia stopped, so too did Harry's heart, reverting instead to the chaotic and ineffective fibrillation that showed up as an erratic, squiggly line on the monitor. If Harry were to survive he needed more advanced lifesaving measures. Tearing open the defibrillator pads with her teeth as she systematically bagged him, Olivia charged the monitor and placed the pads on his chest.

Narelle was now all over Harry, shaking his limp shoulders, kissing his grey cheeks, begging him not to die.

'Narelle, stand back. I need to shock him.' Despite the firmness of her tone and the obvious direness of the situation, Narelle ignored her pleas, and Olivia was left with no choice but to physically drag the hysterical woman off her dying husband and practically throw her onto the couch.

She left Narelle there, sobbing piteously, as she applied the paddles and shocked her patient. The squiggly line remained. Olivia gave him a couple more breaths of oxygen and massaged his chest as she waited for the defibrillator to recharge to a higher setting. Shocking him for a second time, she held her breath and watched the monitor.

Her natural nursing instinct meant that her desire for this stranger to live was heartfelt and genuine, but the thought of being left alone with Narelle and a body if the resuscitation was unsuccessful was also on her mind as she watched the flat line on the monitor with mounting trepidation. But just as Olivia was about to recommence her resuscitation, the monitor flickered as it picked up Harry's heartbeat again. It was slow and irregular at first, but gained in momentum until his output was good and he had started to groan and thrash about, disorientated and in obvious pain. Olivia replaced the ambu-bag with an oxygen mask and lowered her face to his.

'It's all right, Harry,' she said in his ear, her tone gentle and soothing. 'Your heart went into a funny rhythm, but it's beating normally now. I need you to lie very still.'

Harry nodded faintly while Narelle, noticeably calmer but in shock, muttered something about going to fetch water.

Olivia reached for her mobile. She didn't have any choice. Her hands were shaking so much she could hardly manage the tiny keys, but luckily she got straight through.

'Melbourne City Hospital.'

Olivia swallowed hard. 'This is Sister Olivia Morrell.'

'Sister Morrell, it's good to hear—'

'I'm out bush with a critically ill patient. I need some urgent medical advice. Can you put me straight through to Tony Dean?' It was an instruction, not a question and for once Switchboard didn't argue. In an instant she heard Tony Dean's welcomely efficient voice.

'Olivia, where are you?'

She relayed her address with the help of a much calmer Narelle.

'I've got a sixty-eight-year-old man, no previous. Half an hour of chest pain. His ECG showed ST elevation. He went into a VF arrest. I've shocked him twice, and got him back, but...' Olivia glanced over to the monitor, alarmed at the sudden irregularity of his heart rhythm. 'He's throwing off a lot of ectopics. His heart rate's around 45. I'm worried he's going to arrest again. I'm trying to get hold of Clem, his GP, and an ambulance has been called, but that could take ages.'

'You're working for Jake Clemson?'

To Olivia the question seemed entirely irrelevant, but she knew Tony Dean too well to make a smart reply. He wouldn't be wasting time with niceties. 'Yes.'

'Well, that means you'll have everything you need in an emergency pack.'

'But I can't just go ahead and give him drugs without—'

'Yes, you can. This is a life-threatening situation and you're liaising with an emergency consultant.' He spoke very clearly and Olivia knew without a doubt that Tony Dean would face head on any medical legal consequences that might arise and would defend her to the hilt.

'Give him a bolus dose of lignocaine—that will help with the ectopics—and start a sodium bicarbonate infusion. He needs some morphine for pain. You know what you're doing, Olivia. You know the scene, and you've done it a thousand times. Just pretend you're in Casualty with a very incompetent junior doctor and you have to tell them what to do.'

And that was exactly what she did—and it worked. Suddenly she was in complete control, running the show. Looking down at Harry, she gave him a wink. 'You're going to be all right now.' And when Harry managed the tiniest wink back Olivia just knew that he really was.

Tony Dean stayed on the phone, organising the air ambulance from his end, leaving Olivia free to deal with her patient. When the road ambulance arrived she confidently said farewell to Tony, knowing Harry was in the best hands now. The crew worked efficiently alongside Olivia, ensuring Harry was pain-free and stabilising him for his transfer to the base hospital. Through it all Narelle held Harry's hand, whispering words of love and encouragement. Betty had arrived and was outside awaiting the air ambulance. The entire place, in fact, was a picture of quiet efficiency when Clem burst in, somewhat breathless.

'I came as soon as I heard.'

Picking up the ECG tracing, he squeezed the old man's hand.

'G'day there, Harry. What's been going on?' he asked Olivia.

'A myocardial infarction.' Clem nodded and Olivia continued, 'He arrested about five minutes after I got here. I shocked him twice and he reverted to sinus rhythm but he was throwing off a lot of ectopics. I liaised with Tony Dean as I couldn't get hold of you. I gave him a bolus of lignocaine, 5 mg of morphine and a sodium bicarbonate infusion. The ambualnce officers also gave—'

'Anything for nausea?' Clem interrupted.

'Some Maxolon, and I—'

Again Clem interrupted her. 'Good. I'll arrange an air ambulance.'

'It's on its way. They should be here soon.'

'We should give him some aspirin.'

'He's had that.'

For a second Olivia was worried she might be in trouble. Tony Dean, she had no doubt, would back her, but Clem?

He was an unknown entity. But the appreciative smile that crept onto his worried face answered her nagging doubts.

'I didn't need to rush, then, did I, Harry? Livvy had it all under control. It looks like you've been in the best of hands.'

'She's been marvellous,' Narelle enthused. 'Sister, I'm so sorry. I was no help. I just panicked when I saw him like that, I didn't know what to do. Sister had to drag me off him,' she explained to an attentive Clem.

'The air ambulance is in sight,' Betty shrieked from the doorway, destroying in an instant the calm aura that had prevailed. The flurry of activity continued until Harry was safely on his way to the coronary care unit at the base hospital and his niece had arrived to drive Narelle there.

'All in a day's work,' Olivia reflected, as she packed up her box and carefully disposed of the needles and syringes she had used into the small yellow sharps container. Afternoon rounds still had to be done and any earlier intentions of a gourmet meal soon disappeared once she finally made it home and surveyed her fridge.

Not for the first time since arriving at Kirrijong Olivia yearned for the convenience of a local take-away or even a decent deli. She hadn't arrived home till six-thirty and, as it was Ruby's day off, by the time she'd had a quick tidy up it was nudging seven. How she longed to throw a ready-made lasagne in the oven and spend an hour in the bath and put on some make-up. Instead, she hastily browned some mince and threw in some of Alex Taylor's home-made tomato sauce, praying that it would be as good as Alex had promised.

Gargling with asprin for the fourth time that day, she pondered whether to get Clem to take a look at her throat. Perhaps she needed antibiotics.

A quick shower and she faced the mirror. The usually

sleek red hair had curled from the shower steam and framed her flushed face in a wild mass of Titian ringlets.

'What am I doing?' With a jolt she realised she was treating this more like a date than a simple meal between two colleagues. The aspirin wasn't helping much. Her cheeks were burning and every bone in her body ached. Resting her hot face against the cool, smooth mirror, she started to calm down. So maybe she did fancy him, just a bit, and who could blame her? He was undeniably good-looking and working so closely…

'Stop it, stop it,' she reprimanded herself. Hadn't that been one of Jeremy's excuses? She was just being stupid. Anyway, who needed the complications? 'Not me, that's for sure,' she reminded herself firmly. He was her boss, no more, and anyway hadn't she vowed she was off men?

For the first time in years she left off her make-up and pulled on some denim shorts and a plain T-shirt. She certainly didn't want him to think she'd made any effort. If only Olivia had known that when Clem arrived, bringing with him a bottle of red wine and a tub of wickedly fattening double chocolate chip ice cream, his startled expression wasn't, as she assumed, one of disapproval.

Instead, as she opened the door he caught his breath in amazement at the stark contrast to the sophisticated, glamorous woman he was becoming so used to. The sheer natural beauty that radiated from her was truly terrifying; she looked about eighteen. The gorgeous riot of curls that fell in a wild tangled mass onto her slender shoulders gave a warm glow to her face. Without make-up her features were so much more delicate. Clem very nearly flung the ice cream and wine at Olivia and beat a hasty retreat to the safety of his own house. How, he tried to fathom, could he not have noticed how truly beautiful she was?

But he didn't run. He marched through in his usual arrogant way, muttering something about the 'bloody mozzies', and started poking about her kitchen drawers, trying to locate the corkscrew. Olivia added the pasta to the boiling water and busied herself stirring the sauce and cutting up some bread. Finally, just as the small talk had run out, the pasta was ready, and with the aid of a couple of glasses of wine the conversation started to flow. Of course, they talked shop. Olivia noticed how Clem's face lit up when he spoke about children. Many times she had marvelled at his skill to calm the most terrified child or distressed baby.

'I called in on Jean Hunt today. Young Sam is going great guns. She's still breastfeeding, with the odd bottle in the evening. Jean's singing your praises. You should call in, you won't recognise her. Perhaps you could do Sam's twelve-week assessment.'

'I will.' She nodded. Gradually he was handing over more and more to her and she revelled in it. She was already doing the weekly antenatal clinic and was thrilled to be using her midwifery skills, awaiting with anticipation the next delivery, which he had agreed would be hers. Despite her earlier trepidation, she wasn't nervous at the prospect. She couldn't have asked for a better assistant than Clem—he was a paediatrician after all. 'Don't you miss it? Paeds, I mean.'

'Definitely. There's something so rewarding about looking after children. They're so amazingly resilient and uplifting. Even the sickest ones manage to give you something back—a smile, a picture. You're never lonely when you're on the kids' ward.'

He spoke with such passion Olivia couldn't help but probe further. 'Have you ever thought about taking it up again?'

'I think about it every day,' he answered with simple honesty.

'Then why don't you?' It sounded straightforward

enough, but Clem stared at his plate and then looked up at her with a smile she was sure was false.

'Isn't that the six-million-dollar question?'

They moved through to the lounge for dessert. Olivia felt very decadent. Any meal at Jeremy's had always been eaten at the table so as not to mark the furniture. So instilled was this into her, even now she ate her morning toast alone there. Scraping the tub, he offered her the last of the ice cream. Olivia declined. 'No, you have it.'

He shook his head. 'I couldn't eat another thing. That was fabulous, Livvy. Is there no end to your talents?'

'Well, actually,' Olivia confessed, 'I can't take credit for dinner. The pasta is courtesy of Mrs Genobile for dressing her varicose ulcer and the sauce is from Alex for suturing his hand.'

Clem laughed. 'The patients have really taken to you.'

'I've taken to them,' she said honestly. 'The patients here are a lot more appreciative on the whole than the ones in Casualty. Mind you, when you're not waiting six hours on a hard trolley to be seen perhaps it's easier to be gracious.'

'I admitted I missed paeds, now it's your turn. Do you miss it?'

Olivia thought back to her work in Casualty. The team-work, the comradeship. No matter how busy or how tragic the situation there was always time for each other, whether it was a sympathetic chat or a sudden burst of zany hysterics to lighten the mood. It seemed a world away and suddenly she was hit with such a huge wave of homesickness it threatened to drown her. She wondered if she'd ever be amongst them again. She nodded. 'I miss it a lot. That's not to say I'm not happy here,' she added hastily. He was her boss after all. 'But, like you, I think I'd found my niche, career-wise that is. But Jeremy…' Her voice trailed off, not wanting to bring him up again. She was tired of trying to defend him to Clem.

'Go on,' he insisted.

'I'm sorry I keep going back to Jeremy. You'll think I'm using you as an unpaid counsellor.'

He brushed aside her apologies. 'Talk to me, Livvy, I mean really talk. It might do you some good to let it out.'

'I don't want to sound pathetic.'

Looking into his meditative eyes, Olivia felt hypnotised. He had a way of looking at her that somehow seemed to bring her usual barriers of reservation crashing down, and amazingly she felt herself start to open up.

'There's really not much to tell. The same old story—I loved him and thought he loved me. Then I found out he was seeing someone else. He's living with her now. That was the one thing I held back on. Sure I stayed there more often than not, but I wouldn't move in with him. Not until we were married. Maybe I should have.' Olivia shifted uncomfortably, unaccustomed to sharing such intimacies. 'You surely can't want to hear this. You've enough problems without mine.'

'Let me be the judge of that.'

So she told him, well, bits. Choking on the words as she recounted some of the crueller things Jeremy had said to her, things she could hardly even repeat to herself. And he listened—not judging, not criticising, just listened—and topped up her wineglass, and for the second time in their short history he gave her a tissue.

'The strangest part was right at the end, after he'd said every hurtful thing imaginable and I'd handed in my notice and moved into Jessica's. He did a complete about-turn and asked me to come back to him. To start again and forgive and forget.'

'And what did you say?'

'Nothing. I took this job.'

'Were you scared you might relent?' His insight was amazing. Olivia nodded.

'Five years is a long time, and we really did have some good times. I didn't get engaged lightly. To me it was a heartfelt commitment. Part of me doesn't want to throw it all away. Maybe he has changed and learnt his lesson. Perhaps I should give him another chance. But part of me thinks he's blown it. I don't think I could ever really forgive him, ever really trust him again. It's over.'

Clem took her hands. 'Livvy, I hear you when you say it's over, but reading between the lines I can't help thinking you're considering taking him back. I'm sure if it's what you really want then you'll get back with Jeremy, but think hard. You know the saying, "Be careful what you wish for, it may come true." Yes, he might say he's changed and he might mean it for a while. But if he's serious about getting you back, what's he doing, living with Lydia? Shouldn't he be doing his damnedest to show you he's changed?' Clem's face was only inches away, his voice lulling her.

'That's what my mum says, but he really isn't as bad as I've made him out to be,' Olivia replied, suddenly defensive. 'I'm hardly objective, a woman scorned and all that.' She laughed bitterly.

'All I know,' he said gently, still holding her slender hands, 'is that when I had Kathy here, no matter what the circumstances, my main concern above all else was her. Love is about trust. It should make you feel secure, happy and content. Love should make you feel loved. It would have never even entered my head to look at another woman no matter what our problems, and we had our share, I can assure you. But we were a team.'

Olivia saw his eyes mist over and his beautiful full mouth fight for control. She wanted to comfort him but she didn't know how, scared that if she put her arms around his shoulders he might think she was coming on to him. Damn Jeremy, she thought. He had left her so twisted and screwed up she didn't even know how to respond to a friend in anguish.

'Does time heal at all?' she asked. And they knew her question was meant for them both.

'Well, "they" tell me it does. And sure, I'm not the wreck I was in the first few months after Kathy died. There's an old retired doctor in the next town, Dr Humphreys, and there's many a time he had to take over as I was in too much of a state to carry on. But gradually I pulled myself together and, apart from the occasional lapse, I'm in control or appear to be. But not an hour goes by when I don't think of her. Yesterday I went into the basement to find something and I found an old jumper of hers. I could still smell her…' His voice broke. 'Every night I get into bed and there's a huge space where Kathy should be.' His hands covered his face and Olivia was sure she could see the glimmer of tears between his fingers. 'She was too young, Livvy, she shouldn't be dead.'

Olivia sat there frozen, scared to speak in case she started crying, scared to touch him and, more alarmingly, scared of the feelings he stirred in her. In a stilted voice to hide the wave of emotion she felt, she searched for an answer to his dilemma. 'Have you considered moving away, starting afresh, getting away from all the memories?' Olivia felt a jolt inside—the thought of him leaving horrified her. Taking a gulp of wine, she forced herself to focus on the conversation and try to ignore the sudden shift in her feelings towards him. She would analyse them later.

'Well, there's a can of worms.'

'What do you mean?'

'My father's dream was that I'd take over from him as the town GP. Between my brother Joshua and me, I was the safer bet. While Joshua was off backpacking around Asia, calling himself a photographer, I was up to my neck in medical books. It was all I ever intended to do. But after medical school I did my hospital internship and I literally fell in love with paediatrics.

'I was doing very well. I'd just completed my exams and had been made registrar when Mum died suddenly and Dad literally fell to pieces. A case of history repeating itself. I came back to help out and that's when I fell in love with Kathy. Dad just faded away, he died of a broken heart. Kathy never wanted to leave here, but that's another story.'

He stopped talking suddenly and took a long drink. 'I think that's quite enough about me for one night and as for you, young lady, you look as if you're about to drop. Are you sure you're feeling all right?'

Olivia sensed there was a lot more he wasn't telling her. 'Oh, I'll be fine. Just a bit of a sore throat.' That was an understatement. Her throat was killing her.

'I think you'd better get off to bed—doctor's orders.'

'Oh, well, in that case...' She smiled and stood up. Their eyes met and held. Olivia caught her breath, watching transfixed she saw his pupils dilate as his face moved towards her. She could feel his rough chin, feel his mouth on hers. It wasn't a long kiss, just a gentle, unrushed, goodnight kiss, but it held promise and a passion Olivia was scared to interpret. She swayed slightly. Clem caught her wrist.

'Hey, you're really not well.'

'I just stood up too quickly.' She tried to catch her breath, wondering if she'd misread the kiss for he was talking quite normally, apparently unaware of the effect he'd had on her.

'Why don't you take tomorrow off?'

Olivia shook her head. 'I'll be fine, honest.'

'Well, at the very least have a lie-in. Come in a bit later—we'll manage.'

'I couldn't do that. I've got this frightful boss, you see. You just wouldn't believe the fuss he makes if—'

'Hey, hey.' He laughed. 'I really am sorry about this

morning. I can't promise it won't happen again, though, but I will try. I don't ever want to make a promise to you and break it. I always keep my word.'

She knew he was talking more about Jeremy than this morning's incident, and the strangest thing of all, considering her total distrust in men, was that she really believed him.

'I'm sure you do,' Olivia replied.

He moved towards her again, all the time gazing deeply into her eyes. This time there was no mistaking his intention. He was going to kiss her properly. She could feel her pulse pounding in her temples as his warm hands tenderly cupped her face, igniting a passion that, however unexpected, was welcomely received.

But before his full, sensual lips met hers the urgent sound of his pager rudely interrupted the sensual spontaneity of the moment. Its incessant tones took a few moments to register and Olivia opened her eyes abruptly, shaken by what had taken place. Trembling, she sat down as he picked up the phone and punched in a number.

'Do you know what time it is?' The abruptness of his voice made her look up. Clem never spoke to his patients like that, only his staff, she thought cynically. 'Look, Charlotte, it's been a long day. I'm tired.' He looked over at Olivia and rolled his eyes.

Olivia managed a small smile but her mind was whirring. Charlotte. She'd forgotten about her, and now here she was, trying to get hold of Clem at eleven o'clock at night. They must be an item after all. Feelings of shame swept over her. Had she inadvertently been doing to Charlotte what Lydia had done to her?

Clem dropped the phone back into the cradle. 'Look, I'm sorry. I'm going to have to rush off.'

'Nothing serious, I hope?' She was fishing now, secretl

hoping—and feeling cruel for doing so—that his answer would indicate that Charlotte was unwell—a patient.

'No. Just some personal business,' he answered evasively. 'Thanks for dinner.'

There was her answer.

Her composure completely restored, Olivia stood up. 'It was my pleasure. Goodnight, Clem. See you at work.'

The intimacy had faded in an instant.

As he got to the door he turned. 'Look after that throat,' he said, and then he was gone.

Closing the door behind him, Olivia let out a sigh. That had been far too close for comfort. If Charlotte hadn't rung when she had who knew what could have happened.

Taking a couple more aspirin, Olivia crawled into bed. For a moment she closed her eyes and allowed herself the luxury of remembering the feeling of being held in Clem's arms. It had been so long since she had felt wanted. So long since a man had looked at her with lust instead of loathing, compassion instead of contempt.

'No!' She banged her fists on the bed. Clem would be with Charlotte by now. Men—they were all as bad as each other, and she wouldn't let herself forget it again. As far as she was concerned, this night simply hadn't happened.

Turning off the light, she finally drifted off into an uneasy sleep.

CHAPTER FOUR

HAD Olivia been even remotely worried about facing Clem she didn't have time to dwell on it, for the bedside phone awoke her from a restless sleep in the early hours. Fumbling, she picked up the receiver. Knowing the call would be work-related, it forced her mind to concentrate as she flicked on the bedside lamp.

'Livvy, it's Clem. I know I said the next one would be yours but it happened in rather a rush.'

Instantly she was awake, reaching for her pen and note-book in case he was going to give her an address, as she tried to make sense of what he was saying.

'Did I wake you?' he barked.

She glanced at the bedside clock. 'Well, it is two in the morning. Is everything all right?'

'Helen Moffat just delivered, three weeks before her due date,' he explained. 'It was very quick. The baby seemed fine at first, but now I'm just a bit concerned. She's not holding her temperature and her blood sugar is a bit low. I don't want to overreact and get an ambulance, but I do think we ought to keep a closer eye on her. Could you open up the surgery and set up the incubator? I'll bring her over.'

'Sure. I'll be right there.'

Jumping out of bed, Olivia dressed quickly. She might as well put on her uniform as she was obviously going to be there a while. Pulling a comb through her hair, now even more wild and curly, she twisted it into a knot and expertly tied it on her head. She brushed her teeth, put on a slick of lipstick and ran the short distance to the surgery.

The incubator only needed plugging in, as it was always

made up and ready for any such emergency. Clem had said the baby's blood sugar was low so she prepared a paediatric burette and had a flask of dextrose in case the infant needed an infusion.

There was no doubt that the treatment room was impeccably equipped. In fact, many of the monitors here were more up to date than the ones she had used in Casualty. Olivia knew Clem fought tooth and nail to ensure his patients were given the best health care, despite the fact there was no hospital within easy access.

Sure, the town got behind him and arranged fund-raisers for various pieces of equipment, but from what she had seen and heard, a lot came from Clem's own pocket. He was undoubtedly on a good salary—the sheer volume of patients and procedures he undertook assured that—but he certainly didn't rest on his laurels. Instead, he pumped a lot back into the practice and on nights like this it showed.

Unsure if the mother would be coming, Olivia turned down the most comfortable of the patient trolleys and put on the fan heater, despite the warmth of the night.

Her throat was hurting in earnest now. Opening the drug cupboard she took out some aspirin and swallowed them without water.

'Caught you red-handed!'

Olivia swung round, aghast. Surely Clem didn't think she was stealing drugs? He stood in the doorway, dressed in the same clothes he had left her house in, carrying the newborn wrapped in a huge bundle of blankets.

'They're aspirin,' she said tersely, holding out the silver wrapping for him to inspect, then colouring when she saw Clem was laughing.

'Don't be so paranoid,' he teased, then in a more concerned voice added, 'Is that throat of yours no better?'

'It's nothing for you to worry about, though I had better put on a mask—this little lady has enough to contend with without my germs. Where's Helen?' Tying the paper mask, she walked over. Clem had a slightly euphoric manner about him, which at first she put down to too much Charlotte. But remembering her time on a labour ward, she realised with disquieting relief that his mood was more likely to be elevated from the delivery.

'At home. I gave her pethidine, not realising this little lady was going to make such a rapid entrance. She had a good cuddle with the babe while I stitched her, but I think she deserves to sleep it off in bed rather than on one of our hard trolleys.' Clem grinned as she peered into the swag of blankets. 'Livvy, at this ungodly hour anyone else would be wearing jeans and an inside-out T-shirt, yet you manage to look as if you're ready for a day's work. Do you sleep in your uniform?'

'I like to look smart. It's better for the patients,' she replied primly.

'Well, as your patient's only an hour old, I'm sure she'd forgive you if you weren't looking your best. I bet under that mask you're wearing lipstick.'

He was right, of course, but she wasn't going to let him know. 'Don't be silly,' she chided, lowering her eyes, glad the mask was covering her face. She really was useless at lying.

'Well, say hello to Kirrijong's newest resident. Isn't she gorgeous?' Gently he placed the baby in the incubator and unwrapped her. She really was a beautiful baby with an angry look about her pink face which seemed to say, Would you please just leave me alone?

'She's a bit jittery,' Olivia observed.

'It was a very quick labour. I think she's a bit stunned, and she's not very big. Five and a half pounds,' he added. Olivia tried to convert the figures in her head as she pricked the baby's heel to measure her blood sugar. 'Don't make me feel old,' Clem winced. 'Two and a half kilos.'

'That's better.'

'What's her sugar now? I gave her some dextrose back at the house.'

'Four.'

'Fine. We'll check it again in an hour.'

Olivia checked the baby's temperature with the scanner. 'Her temp's still a bit low.'

Clem nodded. 'I'm sure she's fine, though. A few hours' rest in the incubator will do it. We'll check her obs hourly. If she doesn't hold her temp and sugar I'll get her admitted, but I don't think there's any need at this stage. She doesn't need any more glucose for now but we'll push the feeds. There's some sachets of formula and bottles here.' He looked over at her. 'And before you tell me off, Mrs Moffat has already had a nurse and is coming over to feed the baby first thing in the morning. It would seem she's as keen on breastfeeding as you are.'

'I wasn't going to say anything,' Olivia retorted.

'I know. I'm only playing. Why don't you go back to bed, grab a couple of hours while you can?'

Olivia shook her head. 'No. Why don't you? I'll be fine. I'm up now anyway. I'd never get back to sleep.'

He was about to argue, but the thought of bed was far too tempting. 'Are you sure? We could take it in shifts. If I'm back by six you could go home, have a rest and then start a bit later.'

Olivia nodded, for a moment tempted to remind him of yesterday's temper tantrum, but she knew he felt awful enough already, without her rubbing it in.

'You're a godsend, but call me if you're at all concerned. I'm only down the hall.'

Preparing the bottles, Olivia tried not to dwell on the fact that Clem was lying on a bed only a matter of metres away. While it was very reassuring medically speaking, Olivia tried to ignore the pleasantly disturbing feelings the thought evoked. Resolutely she turned her mind away—that was one path she was definitely not going to be taking. Instead, she focused all her attention on the new baby, which was definitely far safer.

Olivia really didn't mind staying up. Making herself a cup of coffee, she settled into the reclining armchair they often used for older patients who were having a dressing and couldn't make it onto the trolley.

She had done her midwifery training at twenty-one, but more for a feather in her cap than any great vocational yearning. It had certainly come in useful on the odd occasion, but at that young age the agony of birth, the swollen breasts and hormone-induced tearful moods had seemed so alien.

Now, however, as her biological clock had started to tick more loudly, she could appreciate so much more what it was all about. Despite her aversion to the labour and post-natal wards, she had always loved the nursery. Loved looking at the tiny newborns, sucking on their fat fists, with nothing to worry about except their next feed, their whole lives ahead of them.

She recognised, too, that adrenaline rush Clem had obviously had from the delivery. Bringing a new life into the world. There was nothing more intimate or magical than that. Maybe it was something she could think about. Perhaps she could do a refresher course and this time around really enjoy midwifery.

She had checked the baby's obs and given her a feed by the time Clem came back, his black hair tousled and his clothes rumpled. 'Thanks for that, I really needed a sleep. How has she been?'

'Good. Her sugar was just on three. I've given her a bottle and her temperature's normal. She seems fine, but the feeds exhausted her. Were Helen's dates right? She's acting just like premmie.'

'I'm sure that's it. Mrs Moffat didn't want to go to the base hospital for a scan so I had to go by her dates. I think the baby's probably more likely thirty-five or -six weeks, than thirty-seven weeks gestation. She's just going to need a lot of small, frequent feeds and be kept warm. We'll keep an eye on her for the rest of the morning, and if she has any further episodes I'll get her admitted.'

'Do you want a coffee?' Olivia offered.

'I'll get it. You go and grab some shut-eye. Don't bother coming in till ten.'

'But you'll need to shower and change. Who'll watch her?' Olivia asked.

'I'll get Betty to come in early, she can keep an eye out. It's not as if the baby's very sick. Rest assured, if there are any problems Betty won't hesitate to pull me out of the shower. She's done it before.'

Olivia raised her eyebrows. 'Now, there's a picture I don't want to dwell on—Betty dragging you out of the shower!'

Clem laughed. 'Betty didn't seem to mind, though I was rather embarrassed, I have to admit. Not because Betty saw me naked, more in the sure knowledge that the whole of Kirrijong would hear about it in all too graphic detail.'

Olivia laughed with him. 'I'll be off, then.' She hesitated for a second. Her body ached for her bed, yet a part of her was reluctant to leave the cosiness of the temporary nursery and Clem in this good humour. Still, what else could she do? There was no reason for her to stay. No logical one anyway.

Her morning shower did nothing to refresh her, but despite feeling awful Olivia dragged herself to work. Her throat felt like sandpaper and every joint in her body ached. She didn't want Clem thinking she was being slack or, more to the point, she didn't want him thinking she was remotely affected by the events of the night before. She needn't have worried. His pleasant mood had evaporated and the night's happenings were evidently history. And that's the way you want it, she reminded herself firmly.

Baby Moffat was fine and slept peacefully. The surgery was unusually quiet and the morning dragged on endlessly, broken only by the occasional blood test and the baby's obs and feeds. Olivia took the opportunity to attack the chaotic cupboards in the treatment room and attempt to get them into some sort of order, but her heart wasn't really in it. Finally, at eleven, Clem checked the baby over and allowed her to go home to her parents, with strict instructions and regular home visits.

Listlessly Olivia washed down the incubator and prepared it for its next customer.

'Are you sure youse should be here?' Betty enquired gently.

'I'm fine,' Olivia replied with more conviction than she felt.

Betty bustled about, tidying magazines and watering the wilting plants. 'Fine, my foot. Youse should be in your bed. I can go and tell Clem—he'll understand. He's very good if his staff need a sickie.'

'No, don't,' Olivia replied, a little too sharply. Betty raised a quizzical eyebrow. 'I'll speak to him myself. I might give afternoon rounds a miss, and catch up tomorrow.'

'Well, if you're sure. I'm finished for the day but it's no problem for me to tell him before I go.'

'No,' Olivia replied firmly. 'You go home, have a good afternoon.'

As Betty fetched her bag Charlotte appeared, just as beautiful as the day before. Olivia flushed, unable to meet the other woman's eyes.

'Can I help you?'

Charlotte almost imperceptibly screwed up her tiny nose. Olivia was positive that she'd had a nose job.

'Where's Clem?' Charlotte asked Betty, completely ignoring Olivia.

'He's in the study,' Betty answered tartly.

Charlotte flounced off, leaving behind a heavy scent of expensive perfume, but as she got to the doorway she turned around and for the first time finally addressed Olivia. 'You could fetch Clem and I some coffee.' And with that she strode off, leaving Olivia standing open-mouthed, staring at her very trim departing backside.

'Ooh, she brings out the worse in me, that one. I dunno what the doctor sees in her,' Betty fumed.

'She and Clem are an item, then?' Olivia had to know.

'It would seem so. Nothing official, like. But she's forever ringing him up and dropping in, and I know they go out when she's in town. They used to date before Clem started courting young Kathy. She must be turning in her grave now that vamp's back on the scene. Not that it's any of my business who he sees, but I tell youse this much—the day she moves in I resign. The thought of seeing that sour face every morning would put me off me cornflakes.'

'But she's very beautiful.' Olivia didn't want Betty to even get a hint that she could be remotely interested in Clem.

'No, sweetie, beauty is from within and that one is as hard as nails. The grief of losing Kathy has turned him if he can't see what a nasty piece of work she is.' And muttering furiously, she bustled off.

Olivia was glad to see the back of her. While she could happily listen for hours on end to Ruby's endless tales and scandals, there was something about Betty's incessant gossiping that irritated her.

Olivia knocked at the study door. Clem looked up surprised when he saw her carrying in the laden tray.

'You didn't have to do that. You're not the housekeeper.'

Charlotte didn't say anything, just sat there puffing on her cigarette.

'You look awful,' Clem stated bluntly.

'Thanks very much,' Olivia muttered.

'Let me take a look at you. We'll go down to the surgery.'

'There really isn't any need. If it's all right, though, I'd rather go home. I've no urgent house calls, and you said you wanted to check on baby Moffat yourself. I can catch up tomorrow.'

'We'll see how you are first. I really think you ought to let me take a look at your throat.'

'I'd rather just go home,' Olivia answered firmly, aware of Charlotte's exaggerated yawn.

'Very well. But go straight to bed and if you feel any worse I want you to call me.'

Olivia nodded and thankfully left the stuffy confines of the study.

Emptying the contents of her handbag onto the bedroom floor, Olivia, with a thermometer under her tongue, searched frantically for some aspirin. 'Some nurse you are,' she muttered to herself. It was no use. She would have to go back to the surgery and get some, but the thought of facing Charlotte and Clem together unnerved her. The chemist's was only a fifteen-minute drive. If she left now she could be there and back in bed within half an hour. Looking at the thermometer, she was alarmed to see how high her temperature was. Oh, well, there was nothing else for it. Grabbing her purse and keys from the floor, she ran out to the Jeep.

Olivia decided to take the short cut Clem had shown her when she'd first arrived. It was along an unsealed road and would eventually take her out at the turning for town. That way, at least Clem wouldn't see her driving off. She was supposed to be sick after all.

'This is ridiculous,' she scolded herself as the four-wheel-drive bumped along the rough terrain. 'Behaving like some fugitive when I'm only nipping out for some aspirin.' A nagging voice told her she was in no fit state to be driving but she didn't realise it was the fever that was making her act so rashly. Clinging to the wheel, she wished she'd taken the main road. Clem had managed to make it look so easy, but in her present state she wasn't up to advanced driving skills.

Suddenly the vehicle spluttered, jolting a couple of times, and then stopped. Frantically she turned the key in the ignition—nothing. With mounting panic she pumped her foot on the accelerator—still nothing.

'Damn, damn,' Olivia cursed as she checked the fuel gauge. It read empty. She let out a small wail of horror. Of all the stupid things to have done. She had always been so meticulous. What was happening to her? First running out of aspirin, now petrol—and here of all places. She pictured her mobile telephone lying useless on the floor at home, along with the rest of her handbag contents. Gripping the steering-wheel, she fought to regain control. 'Don't panic,' she told herself firmly. 'Think.' It was no big deal. She could walk to the garage. It couldn't be that far.

Getting out of the vehicle, Olivia eyed the endless road ahead. There was no way she could walk it—that would take for ever and in her present state she simply wasn't up to it. Perhaps she should just wait. Surely someone would come along soon. But who? Clem had said that practically no one used this road. What if she were to cut through the bush? That would take ages off the journey and would bring her onto the main road. She couldn't just sit here and do nothing. Olivia tentatively stepped off the road and into the scrub. It wasn't that dense and if she just kept heading in the right direction she would be there in no time. Once on the main road someone would give her a lift.

Purposefully she walked, ducking branches, the eerie silence broken only by her own breathing and the snapping of twigs as she stepped on them. Suddenly something warm brushed her leg and Olivia let out a scream. A possum, which had been happily feasting on some berries until she had disturbed him, stood there frozen with fear. For a second he stared at Olivia with terrified eyes and then shot up the nearest tree. The incident was over in seconds, but it was all it took to unnerve her, and in that instant she lost her bearings.

For a few minutes she wandered in circles, frantically trying to find a familiar landmark, something she recognised, but it was useless. Finally, overwhelmed and exhausted, Olivia's legs gave way and she lay on the rough forest floor. How could she have been so stupid? She was really in trouble now. Who was going to find her? No one even knew she was out here. Clem thought she was safely tucked up in bed. Even if he did somehow notice that she was gone, he was hardly going to come out looking for her, let alone here.

Her face was burning, her throat so swollen she could hardly swallow. Olivia could hear the kookaburra's laughing in the treetops. Laughing at her for being so silly to think she might get Jeremy back, laughing at the stupid city girl who had got herself well and truly lost.

The hours limped by and finally her eyes grew too heavy to keep open, the urge to sleep, just for a little while, tempting. Perhaps she would wake up with renewed energy and start again. But she resisted the urge, terrified of waking up only to still be here. As night drew in, though, too scared to stay awake and listen to the animals' shrieking, Olivia gave in to temptation and let sleep wash over her.

How long she lay there she wasn't sure, but the sound of footsteps woke her. 'Over here,' she croaked, terrified her voice would desert her and she might be missed. A torch shone brightly in her face, making her put her hands up to shield her eyes from the sudden light.

'What the hell are you playing at, you bloody idiot?' There was no mistaking Clem's angry voice.

She felt so ill and cold, and totally, utterly, humiliated. 'I'm sorry, I didn't feel well,' was all she could manage to rasp.

'So you drove off into the middle of nowhere and went for a bush walk?' Clem demanded.

Her head was spinning, sweat drenching her. 'I went to get some aspirin.' Olivia tried feebly to explain.

Clem, relief and fear making him shout, realised this wasn't the time to be reprimanding her. This woman was sick. 'It doesn't matter now,' he said more gently. 'Come on, Livvy, let's get you home.'

And suddenly it all hit her. Whether it was because of her raging temperature, or the weeks of agony Jeremy had put her through, or a deep-rooted longing for her family in England, a huge surge of loneliness and desperation hit her like a bolt of lightning and she let down the guard she had fought so hard to keep up. 'What home?' she croaked. 'I haven't got a home. Nobody wants me.'

'Hush now.' Clem cradled her in his arms. 'Things will seem better soon.' He stroked her sodden hair, drenched with sweat, and rocked her gently. Feeling his strong arms around her and the solid weight of his body, for a moment Olivia leant against him, breathing in his familiar scent, allowing herself to be comforted. Gradually the panic in her subsided.

'I'm sorry. I'm fine now,' she gasped, mortified at Clem seeing her like this.

'You're anything but fine.' He fiddled around with a two-way radio and gave some garbled message about locating and retrieving. With horror Olivia realised he was talking about her. There was a search party out after her.

'I ran out of petrol,' she attempted again to explain.

Clem shook his head. 'You never, ever leave your vehicle. If Laura Genobile hadn't been out riding and seen the Jeep, who knows what could have happened to you?' Seeing her sitting there utterly defeated, the anger in Clem, borne from fear, evaporated and he scooped her up in his arms. 'I'll lecture you later.'

She insisted on trying to walk and he half dragged her through the bush, but her legs were too weak and soon gave way. Clem lifted her up and with no strength left to argue, there was no choice other than to let him carry her what was, in fact, just a short distance to his car. Laying her on the back seat, he gently lifted her head and gave her a drink of water and then drove her back home.

Dougie and Ruby were waiting anxiously, and ran out to meet them as Clem carried her into her house. 'Oh, Livvy, where on earth have you been? We've been so worried,' came Ruby's anxious voice as she hovered nervously, while Clem gently lowered her onto the bed.

'She just popped out to get some aspirin,' Clem replied dryly, but the sarcasm in his voice wasn't wasted on Olivia. 'I'm just going to examine her. Perhaps you could find a nightdress, Ruby.'

Olivia sat up, determined to retrieve her dignity and horrified at the thought of Ruby holding up one of her skimpy nightdresses for all to see. 'I'd like a bath first if you don't mind.'

Clem sighed. 'How did I guess that you'd have to argue?' He sounded irritated. 'Very well. Ruby, perhaps you could run a bath, not too warm, and then help her into bed. I'll get my bag and a couple of things from the surgery, then I want to examine her properly.'

After her bath Olivia sat lamely on the edge of the bed, wrapped in a huge towel. The exertion had completely depleted any remaining strength she might have had. Ruby peeled away the towel and Olivia attempted to cover her naked breasts with her arms.

'This is no time for modesty,' Ruby fussed.

Even in her semi-delirious state she managed to feel a glimmer of horror as Ruby lifted her arms and dressed her in a huge, gaudy, pink and purple floral nightdress. 'Where did that come from?' she croaked.

'I prepared your room. Your nightdresses wouldn't cover a sparrow. I didn't want youse feeling embarrassed in front of Clem so I fetched a few of mine—there's some more in your top drawer.' Ruby rubbed Olivia's hair dry vigorously with the towel. 'Right, sweetie, into bed with you.'

Thankfully, she slipped her aching body between the cool crisp sheets and laid her burning head on the soft pillows. She knew she must look an absolute fright, but for the first time in her adult life she couldn't have cared less about her appearance. Remembering her earlier hysterics, Olivia lowered her eyes in embarrassment as Clem entered the room.

'That's better.' He smiled. 'Thank you, Ruby. Perhaps you could make Livvy a warm, milky drink with a bit of sugar. Dougie has just gone to sort out the Jeep.'

'I've put everyone to so much trouble. I'm so sorry.'

'There, there, sweetie.' Ruby's fat hand held Olivia's slender one. 'Don't go getting upset. We're just all glad you're safe. You had us so worried.' Closing the door as she left, Olivia held her breath as Clem walked over to her, sure he was going to scold her, but he didn't say a word. Popping a thermometer into her mouth, he picked up her slim wrist and took her pulse. Olivia glanced up shyly at him.

'One of Ruby's passion-killers?' he said, looking at the

fluorescent gown that smothered her. The sudden unexpected humour caught Olivia by surprise and a small smile flickered over her pale lips. The thermometer wobbled. Taking it out of her mouth, he glanced at it but she couldn't read his expression. Gently he felt her neck. 'When did you start to feel unwell?'

Olivia thought for moment. 'Well, I've been under the weather for a while. I put it down to stress and a new job, but over the last few days I've been feeling a lot worse. I think I've got the flu.'

'I'll decide what's wrong with you,' he stated firmly. 'Your glands are huge. Let me have a look at your throat.'

Olivia obediently opened her mouth, wishing Ruby had let her brush her teeth.

'Ugh,' he said. 'No wonder you feel awful. Now, pull up your nightie. I need to examine your abdomen.'

'But I've got a sore throat,' Olivia protested weakly.

'Livvy, I'm a doctor. Would you feel more comfortable if I asked Ruby to come in?' he offered.

'No, of course not.' It wasn't that she didn't trust him, far from it. She was just all too aware of her painfully skinny body. She had always been on the thin side, but since she had broken up with Jeremy the weight had fallen off her.

Clem helped her to sit up and deftly removed the pillow, gently lowering her till she lay flat on the bed. His large hands gently probed her stomach. Olivia lay there, every muscle in her body rigid, mortified at the embarrassment of it all.

'Relax, Livvy, please,' he urged. 'Are you tender there?'

'No.'

'Or there?' He pushed again.

'No,' she lied.

'Livvy, please, relax your muscles—you're making it impossible for me to examine you. How about there?'

Olivia winced slightly. 'No!' Hastily she pulled down the awful nightdress and sat up. 'Look, I'm fine, I tell you. Now, if you'll just give me some aspirin and let me sleep, I'll be all right.'

'No, you won't.' Replacing the pillow, he held her shoulders and gently eased her back. 'It will need to be confirmed by a blood test, but I'm pretty sure you've got glandular fever.'

Olivia relaxed onto the pillow and closed her eyes. In a funny way it was actually a relief. So that's what was wrong with her. At least it explained the exhaustion and lethargy. At least there was a reason for the ever-threatening tears. She wasn't losing her mind after all, just struggling against a nasty viral infection. Clem let her digest the news and then continued. 'I was attempting to examine your abdomen for any enlargement of your liver or spleen. You certainly don't make things easy.'

An awful thought suddenly occurred to Olivia. 'I couldn't have infected any of the patients, could I? What about baby Moffat?'

Clem smiled. 'Unless you've been going around town kissing your patients passionately there's nothing to worry about. And if you have,' he added teasingly, 'we'd better have a long talk.'

Not the patients, just the doctors. She blushed as she remembered the previous night. Thank goodness Clem's pager had gone off when it had. Clem must have read her mind, but it didn't take an Einstein to guess what she was thinking.

'I had it myself when I was a student, so I know how rotten you must be feeling,' he said lightly, but the inference was there—she couldn't have given it to him anyway.

'So, what now?' Olivia asked, but she already knew the answer.

'Bed rest, bed rest and more bed rest, and not just because of the glandular fever. I believe you're emotionally exhausted as well as physically, and until you rest and get your strength back you're going to keep picking up every bug around. I'll move you over to my house, where it will be easier for Ruby and I to keep an eye on you.'

'No,' she answered quickly. 'I'll manage fine here.'

'Are you listening to a word I say, or are you just deliberately being difficult?' Clem asked, exasperated. 'Livvy, you have glandular fever. It isn't going to go away in a couple of days, you need to be looked after properly.'

'I said I'll manage,' Olivia replied with as much strength as she could muster.

'Look.' He appeared to relent. 'If you really can't stand the idea of having me looking after you, then perhaps I could arrange for transport to take you back to Melbourne. Is there someone who can care for you there?' Clem felt cruel, saying this, but it really was the last card he had left up his sleeve to play against this most unwilling patient.

Olivia lay there, defeated. Who, indeed? She couldn't dump herself on Jessica again, and all her other friends had jobs and families—they didn't need an emotional wreck with glandular fever to land on their doorsteps. And Jeremy? That was almost laughable. Perhaps she'd end up sharing a house with him and Lydia. Olivia turned her troubled eyes to Clem and shook her head. If she'd expected a look of sympathy she didn't get one.

'Well, then, it looks as if you're stuck with us. I'll compromise, though. You can stay here on the strict condition that you ring if there's the slightest problem, and that Ruby and I can drop in freely. At the first sign that you're doing too much I'll carry you over to the main house myself. Understood?'

Olivia nodded glumly. She wasn't exactly inundated with options.

'Good. Now, try and get some sleep. I'm going to fetch

some paperwork from home and then I'll be back. I'll be in the lounge all night if you need anything.'

Olivia opened her mouth to object. He couldn't stay here. He had surgery in the morning and she knew he had hardly slept last night. Then, remembering his threat of carrying her over to his house, she thought better than to argue. Clem was quite capable of bundling her up in these blankets and taking her over there right this minute. 'Thanks,' she muttered, though not very graciously.

'Now, is there anything I can get you?'

Shaking her head, she watched as he walked to the bedroom door. 'Clem?'

He turned. She wanted to say thank you, for finding her, for caring. And to say she was sorry for all the trouble. But she was scared she might start to cry. What was it about this man that brought her usually hidden emotions bubbling to the surface? 'Could I have another milky drink?'

He gave her a wide smile. 'Oh, no, what have I done? They say nurses make the worst patients.'

For the next forty-eight hours Olivia's dreams were as erratic as her temperature. Jeremy would appear in bed next to her, his lithe, taut body as beautiful as it always had been, whispering endearments, telling her how much he loved her. She would turn and reach out for him but then the door would open and Lydia would be there, carrying huge syringes and saying, 'Trust me, I'm a doctor.' Her husky voice would fill the room. Panicking, Olivia would reach for Jeremy for reassurance, for help, but he would lie there, laughing.

'How could I not want her, darling? Look at yourself— did you really think I would choose you?'

She would wake up screaming, drenched in sweat, desperately trying to escape the hypodermic that Lydia bore, fighting against them both. Within seconds dear Ruby would appear, as solid as a rock, in a vast dressing-gown, her hair in a net. The room would be flooded with light and Olivia would sob into the huge bosom, wishing Ruby were her mother. 'There, there, sweetie, it was just a dream. No worries, just a horrid dream,' the familiar Aussie voice would say. Ruby would stay with her then, dozing in the chair, and Olivia would lie there listening to Ruby's gentle snoring, praying for the morning so she could say she'd got through another night.

By the fourth night her temperature had long since subsided, yet the nightmares stayed. She awoke at two a.m. gripped with the same panic and fear that had haunted her since Jeremy had gone. Jeremy—where was he? Why wasn't he lying there next to her? And then it dawned on her that she was alone and he was with Lydia. This wasn't a nightmare she was having, this was sheer, living hell.

She longed for her mother, longed for the vast oceans that separated them to miraculously disappear and Mum to be there to somehow make things all right like when she was little, to promise things would seem better in the morning. But her mother was in England, as unattainable as Jeremy. The tears fell then, and she didn't fight them, just let the great shuddering sobs that convulsed her body come, doing nothing to hold them back.

Suddenly the light flicked on and she felt comforting hands massaging her shoulders, gently stroking her hair. 'It's OK, Livvy, let it out.'

Olivia froze. Where was Ruby? This was Clem she was weeping on. Abruptly she turned onto her back, pulling the covers up to her chin. 'I'm all right, it was just a dream.' She could feel his solid weight on the bed next to her, feel the warmth of his leg against hers through the thin sheet. What did it matter that it was Clem? At least it was another human being.

'Come here,' he said softly, and opened his arms to her.

She lifted her body slightly and, unresisting, allowed him to pull her towards him, enveloping her in his embrace. His strong arms wrapped tightly around her fragile frame and he held her securely, rocking her gently as she wept, never admonishing her, not once telling her to calm down, until finally the sobs subsided. Clem eased her back onto the pillows, tenderly wiping away her tears with the corner of the sheet. 'You've been through one hell of a lot, but things will get better.'

'Do you really think so?'

'I know so,' he said with conviction. She searched his face. He seemed so positive, so sure, and she badly wanted to believe him. Even before he moved she sensed his departure. As he stood up she felt the coldness of the sheet against her leg without him there.

'Please, don't go.' The words were out before she could stop them.

'I'm not going anywhere, I'm right here.' And sitting himself in the bedside chair, he leant over and turned out the light. 'Try to get some sleep. I'm here if you need me.'

Aware of his powerful presence, comforted by his regular breathing, gradually she drifted off and had the first peaceful sleep she'd had in weeks.

'Clem said you could have a bath today.'

Olivia winced as Ruby flung open the bedroom curtains. The bright morning sun flooded the rumpled bed. She looked around the room, her eyes coming to rest on the chair where Clem had slept, desperately trying to remember what she had said. How could she have let him see her in that state? How could she have lowered her guard like that? It was as if she'd been to a wild party and had a frightful hangover without the pleasure or excuse of champagne. Burying her head under the sheets Olivia frantically tried to piece together just what she had told him. She could vaguely remember the word Jeremy coming up too many times and a speech about her mother, and then pleading with him not to go.

'Oh, God.'

Ruby was over in a flash. 'Livvy, are you all right? Should I fetch Clem?'

'Oh, no, please, don't.' Even the thought of facing Clem made her blush from her head to her toes. Getting up slowly, Olivia made her way gingerly to the bathroom on legs that felt like jelly. Ruby placed a pile of towels and yet another flannelette creation on the vanity unit.

'I'll be right outside. If youse get dizzy call me straight away.'

'I will, I promise.'

Slowly she lowered herself into the huge enamel tub and wallowed in the luxury of the hot, bubbly water. She massaged conditioner into her hair and lay back, letting the water lap over her body. Deliberately she blocked all thoughts of Jeremy and Clem out of her mind, and just relished the moment.

'C'mon, now, sweetie, you don't want to overdo it.'

Exhausted from her exertions, Olivia sat obediently as Ruby dried her hair a few minutes later. 'I think I've got some cotton pyjamas in the dressing-table drawer,' Olivia ventured, crossing her fingers as Ruby scrabbled through her drawers. Sure enough, there they were, under a pile of lingerie.

'I'll go and fix you some breakfast while you get changed, but no hanging around—pyjamas on and then bed.'

Feebly she ran a comb through her hair and tied it in a high ponytail secured with a white scrunchie. Catching sight of herself in the mirror, she screwed up her face at the pale, drawn reflection that stared back. Realising she must be approaching death not to even want to put on make-up, Olivia acknowledged there were some absolute essentials in life and liberally sprayed her wrists and neck with her favourite perfume. Feeling refreshed but exhausted, gratefully she crawled back into the fresh bed Ruby had made up. She soon bustled in, carrying a tray.

'I've made you some toast and scrambled eggs. Now, there's freshly squeezed orange juice, with just a squirt of lemon. Be sure and drink it all, youse need your vitamin C.'

Olivia looked at the laden tray and felt a huge lump in her throat. Dear Ruby, she had made such an effort. She had even picked some anemones from the garden and arranged them in a tiny vase. 'I'll try.'

'You'll do more than try,' Ruby insisted. 'I used to squeeze the oranges and lemons for poor Kathy—she reckoned that was what got her through the mornings.'

The piece of toast in Olivia's hand dropped to the plate. She stared at the untouched orange juice. She knew it was none of her business, but she just had to know. 'What was she like—Kathy?'

The question stopped Ruby in her tracks. Taking a deep breath, she sat on the bed beside Olivia. For a while she didn't say anything, just stared out of the window, then she finally turned.

'She was the best,' she said in an unusually subdued voice. 'I remember her as a little 'un always smiling. She always loved Clem, long before he even noticed her. I remember when he started to date that Charlotte. Kathy's mum told me she cried the whole night through. Then the next thing I heard they were together and I've never seen a couple happier. They loved each other so much. Not that they were gushing or anything like that. It was just so obvious to everyone. They didn't need to tell you, it just showed in their faces. Clem's never been the same, and I don't think he ever will be. There's this sadness in his eyes, always there. He's always thinking of her.'

'How did she die?'

'Cancer. A wicked disease, it's no respecter of age or beauty.' Ruby wiped away a tear that spilled down her fat, rosy cheeks.

'Was she very beautiful?'

'She was a real beaut, our Kathy. Didn't need make-up, she was beaut inside and out. We all loved her. I used to come and sit with her near the end if Clem had to go to an emergency or when we could persuade him to have a sleep. Not once did she complain or worry about herself, just Clem—how he'd cope, who'd look after him. She never once said, ''Why me?'''

Olivia felt the hot tears spill now onto her own cheeks. The two women sat there for a time, both locked in their own private thoughts. Finally Ruby stood up. 'C'mon, Livvy, eat your breakfast now, sweetie. I'll get on.'

Half-heartedly Olivia pushed the toast around her plate. The tears that fell unchecked were for Kathy, the beautiful woman she had never met. Kathy. So cruelly robbed of time, taken for no apparent reason from the people she loved. And they fell for Clem, too. A good man, who didn't deserve this—to be left alone to pick up the pieces without his beautiful wife by his side.

CHAPTER FIVE

GRADUALLY Olivia regained her strength. Ruby, ever diligent, petted and fussed over her like a broody hen, coaxing her to eat the huge meals she prepared, letting her ramble on endlessly and shooing out visitors when she felt it was getting too much.

Not that she had many—a couple of her regular patients dropped in, bearing fruit and chocolates. Iris Sawyer, the retired practice nurse, had been a couple of times, but despite her insistence that the surgery was coping and Olivia should concentrate on getting well, the visits only served to make Olivia feel even more guilty. Iris should be enjoying her retirement, not covering for her. Betty seemed to feel it was her duty to visit daily and fill Olivia in on every last piece of gossip she could glean from the surgery. Olivia found the visits exhausting and was always relieved when Ruby appeared at the bedroom door and suggested Betty join her in the kitchen for a cuppa.

The only person she looked forward to seeing was Clem. He was good company and never demanding. He would sit on the edge of her bed and chat idly about his day or the patients. Sometimes he would bring over the plans for the new hospital, asking her advice on the layout. It was nice to be involved and he always took her suggestions seriously.

'You've just shot our budget for another five grand,' he would say with a laugh as she overhauled the resuscitation area or moved the nurses' station. Other times he would just sit in the armchair and write his notes, the silence never awkward. Sometimes Olivia would drift off to sleep, only stirring when he left as he gently tucked the blankets in around her and put a cool hand on her forehead to check her temperature. He had never told her off about the stupidity of her actions, but she felt a lecture was only a matter of time.

One afternoon as Clem flicked through a medical journal Ruby burst through the bedroom door, her face hidden behind a huge bunch of yellow roses.

'These just arrived for you, Livvy. They must've cost a fortune, there's no florist in town, they had to be sent by courier.' She practically tossed Clem the mail she had collected and then, blatantly indiscreet, hovered by the bed as Olivia, her hands shaking, opened the tiny envelope.

'They're from Jeremy,' she said in an incredulous voice 'How did he know I was sick?'

'That's my fault, I'm afraid.' Ruby at least had the grace to blush. 'He rang a few days ago. He sounded nice and so concerned and I knew how youse was missing him and all.'

'But how did he know I was here?' Olivia asked, bewildered.

'Tony Dean probably told him,' Clem answered logically, without bothering to look up from his mail. 'And I wouldn't be too hard on Ruby. I nearly rang Jeremy myself when you did your disappearing act. You do realise, don't you, that he's on your résumé as your emergency contact?'

Olivia chose to ignore the question and its obvious implications, tears welling in her eyes as she read the card. 'He's coming to see me. He wants to talk.'

'Well, he'd better step on it. If the time his flowers took to get here is anything to go by, you'll be disgustingly healthy and back at work by the time he arrives.' There was no mistaking the harshness in Clem's voice, though all the while he spoke he carried on reading his mail, not even glancing at Olivia or her flowers.

'Don't be like that, Clem. It would have been hard to organise the delivery,' Ruby reasoned, seeing the disappointment flicker in Olivia's eyes.

'I just can't believe he's coming all this way to see me.'

'Neither can I,' Clem replied dryly, then in a gentler tone added, 'Just don't get your hopes up, OK?'

Olivia nodded.

'I'm going for a walk. I'll pop in later this evening.' He stood up and stretched, yawning without bothering to cover his mouth, his untucked shirt lifting with the movement just enough to reveal a glimpse of his muscled stomach. Olivia turned away, suddenly embarrassed.

'You're going already?' She couldn't hide the disappointment in her voice.

'I need some fresh air and I'd better go and check on the builders. There are a few things that need to be sorted—anyway, I expect you've got a bit to think about.' He gestured towards the flowers and then sat down on the bed. His dark eyes turned to her and Olivia felt her pulse rate rise. It was as if he were staring right at her very soul. Shaken, she looked away. Her soul really wasn't up to scrutiny at the moment. 'Please, Livvy, be careful.'

Unable to speak, desperately trying to keep her breathing even, it was all she could do to nod dumbly at him. In that instant she knew beyond a shadow of a doubt that her rising pulse rate and flushed cheeks had nothing to do with the glandular fever. It wasn't only Jeremy she had to be careful about. There was no hiding from it—she felt far more for Clem than she had ever dared admit, a physical attraction so strong she could almost taste it. As he left, gently closing the door behind him, Olivia lay back on the pillow, bewildered and confused at the feelings that coursed through her. The scent of Jeremy's roses seemed to overpower the room, clashing with the lingering musky traces of Clem's aftershave.

'Ignore him, pet. He's in a bad mood because he got a letter from his brother Joshua. He probably wants Clem to send him yet another blank cheque. Youse just enjoy your flowers. He sounds sound like a fine young man, that Jeremy.'

'He had an affair, he's still living with her,' Olivia reminded the elder woman, who had heard the whole story time and again.

'Happen he made a mistake. My Dougie was no angel. Many a tear I shed over his dalliances, but once we were wed, well, he's never looked at another woman,' Ruby said as she tucked in Olivia's bedspread. 'Now, try and get some rest.'

The phone by the bed rang shrilly. Ruby had just gone out.

'Hello.'

'Olivia, darling, is that you?' There was no mistaking the husky voice on the other end.

'Jeremy,' she gasped incredulously. 'I just got your flowers.'

'Sorry I took so long in sending them, but I've been caught up at the hospital.'

In just one short sentence he had incriminated himself. Wasn't his roster always his excuse? If he'd just stayed quiet she could have gone on believing that the flowers had simply been delayed. It was as if a huge alarm bell had sounded in her head.

Be careful, Olivia warned herself, echoing Clem's words from just moments before.

'What can I do for you?' Olivia spoke slowly, playing for time so she could decide how to handle the situation.

'Darling, don't sound so formal. I'm ringing to see how you are, of course. I've been so worried. Tony Dean said you were out bush in Kirrijong of all places, and then I finally track down a number and some old biddy tells me you've got glandular fever. I've been trying to speak to you for ages, but every time I ring some proprietorial bush quack tells me you're resting. I hope they're looking after you all right. Has he checked your liver function and—?'

'I'm being looked after beautifully,' Olivia answered curtly. Far better than you would have, she wanted to add, but she simply wasn't up to a row.

'Oh, well, good. I just wanted to make sure. Some of these country doctors can be a bit old-fashioned—they don't always keep themselves up to date. I just want to know you're getting the correct treatment.'

'Don't be so pompous,' Olivia snapped. How dared he make out Clem was some sort of backwater hick?

'Let's not argue, sweetheart,' he soothed. 'Right now I'm far more interested in finding out when you're coming home.'

Olivia nearly dropped the phone. He was talking as if she might have been delayed at the shops. 'What about Lydia?' She heard his sharp intake of breath.

'You leave her to me, Olivia. I miss you. I was an idiot to ever let you go. I need you, darling.' His voice dropped and slowly, caressingly he whispered endearments, using all the phrases of old that had never failed to win her around.

She lay motionless on the bed, listening, her knuckles white as she gripped the telephone. How did he do it? He had treated her so badly and yet she could feel herself weakening. There was something about his manner, a desperation creeping into his voice that made her think that maybe, just maybe he had changed.

She closed her eyes and for an instant Clem's face flashed into her mind, but she resolutely pushed it away. She mustn't confuse the issue. Clem had Charlotte and, anyway, this was five years of her life they were talking about. Surely that must count for more than some idiotic notion she had only entertained for literally five minutes.

'Are you and Lydia completely finished?' Even before he replied she knew there would be a flood of excuses.

'Darling, she's harder to get rid of than a red wine stain,' he drawled.

'Have you tried salt?' Olivia quipped, but Jeremy wasn't to be deterred.

'Just tell me you're coming home and I'll have her out of here in five minutes flat. She's absolutely obsessed with me, you know. I'm not just making excuses. She pursued me relentlessly, just never let up. I know I should have been stronger, but I was so stressed, what with this interview coming up and us going through a rough patch.'

Her mind whirred. What rough patch? As far as she'd been concerned, there hadn't been any major problems, just the usual dramas Jeremy was so good at creating. No relationship was perfect all of the time. Surely if it had been that serious he should have come to her, tried to work things out, before jumping into bed with Lydia. 'I don't want to hear excuses, Jeremy.'

'Of course you don't. You're not well, I understand that, but things will be better now. We can work this out. Just come back home. I really miss you, darling.'

'It has nothing to do with whether I'm well or not,' Olivia retorted sharply. 'And anyway I've got obligations here.'

'What are you talking about?' Jeremy answered, irritated and somewhat taken back by her refusal. This wasn't going to be as easy as he'd anticipated.

'I've got a job here. I can't just up and leave on a vague promise that you'll get rid of Lydia.' Her voice was rising. How dared he assume she'd drop everything and rush back into his arms?

'What about me?' he wailed like a selfish five-year-old. 'Aren't your obligations to me? I am your fiancé after all.'

'Ex,' Olivia stated resolutely. 'You relinquished your rights when you went to bed with Lydia. Don't try to turn this on me.'

Realising he was on the wrong track, Jeremy changed his tune. 'Olivia, calm down. Please, don't upset yourself. Obviously we can't sort this out in one telephone call, but surely five years together is worth fighting for?' Taking her silence as a positive sign, he continued, 'I was hoping to tell you this over a bottle of champagne but, given the circumstances, I'll tell you now. I know it will cheer you up.'

Olivia lay there, exhausted. What now? Wasn't this enough to be going on with?

'I got it, sweetheart,' he purred into the phone. 'I've been offered the junior consultant position. We're on our way, darling, you and me together. Mr Felix can't wait till you're well enough to go out for a celebratory meal. Things really are changing.'

So that was his plan. Jeremy wanted to dispel any rumours of relationship difficulties to his new boss. And though it would never be said in so many words, wasn't Jeremy now expected to have a wife on his arm at the never-ending round of functions they would have to attend? Was that why he wanted her back? She lay there, not saying a word, just listening to his endless stream of platitudes.

'Don't write us off, Olivia. I made a mistake, sure, but we've had five years together, we can't just let it go. I've been doing a lot of thinking and I've decided you're right. Perhaps it is time to set a date, and then we can start a family, put all this mess behind us.'

He was good. She had to give him that. The sugar to sweeten the bitter pill. Wasn't a baby the one thing she had desperately wanted? But not like this, not a patch job to save a crumbling relationship. She thought of Jean Hunt and how she had fought so hard to keep it all together. What if she had a difficult baby like young Sam? Jeremy would be out the door in a flash.

With every ounce of self-control she could muster, Olivia spoke in clear, even tones. 'Jeremy, the last thing I ever wanted was this ''mess'', as you call it. It was your doing. Do you really think I'd just come back and marry you after what you've put me through?'

'Olivia, please! Just listen—'

'No, Jeremy, *you* listen. Thank you for the flowers, thank you for ringing up to see how I'm doing, and congratulations on your promotion. Now, if you'll excuse me, I'm very tired.' And leaving him spluttering, she hung up and then promptly removed the telephone receiver from the cradle.

Over the next few weeks Jeremy rang regularly. More often than not Olivia let the answering machine take his calls but she occasionally picked up. To his credit Jeremy did seem genuinely sorry for the pain he had caused and it was obvious that he missed her, but Olivia deliberately kept the conversations light, too exhausted for another confrontation. Clem, on the other hand, became more and more distant. Still kind and considerate, he seemed rather formal. It was as if their brief intimacy had never happened and, indeed, Olivia sometimes wondered if she had imagined the whole thing.

Christmas was looming, but this year it held no excitement for her. It only served to ram home her loneliness. She thought glumly of the hospital balls that she was missing, the parties and celebrations. Ruby bustled into town with Olivia's shopping list and she listlessly wrote a few cards, but that was about as exciting as it got.

Late on one particularly long, boring afternoon Jeremy

rang while Clem was visiting. Instead of politely leaving the room, he stayed and carried on writing his notes. Not to be intimidated, and curious about Clem's reaction, Olivia carried on the conversation but Clem didn't appear remotely fazed. Damn him, Olivia thought. She might just as well have been talking to her mother.

Jeremy, on the other hand, unused to such a friendly audience, carried on chatting. Then, as if sensing another man's presence, for the first time Jeremy began to talk more intimately. His husky tones did nothing for her but, catching Clem's eye, Olivia blushed furiously and started to giggle. Clem rolled his eyes, obviously not remotely impressed by her behaviour. Hastily she concluded the conversation.

'You didn't have to hang up on my account,' Clem said curtly as she replaced the receiver.

'I didn't.'

'How's Jeremy?' he asked dryly.

'He seems fine,' Olivia answered noncommittally.

'And Lydia?'

'What do you mean?' How cruel of him to bring her up Olivia thought.

'Well, not so long ago she was the object of Jeremy's desire and the reason for your misery. I just wondered if she was still on the scene.'

She didn't respond. Maybe the phone call had got to him after all.

'You seem a lot better. I was thinking you could go for a little walk tomorrow. It will do you good to get some fresh air.'

Olivia nodded eagerly. It would be great to get out and blow away some cobwebs. 'When can I go back to work?'

'Easy.' He smiled. 'Let's see how you go tomorrow. There's a nice little track that takes you to a clearing by a creek, it's pretty spectacular. Ruby will give you directions, and mind you listen to them. No short cuts, please.'

Olivia blushed. 'I really am sorry about that.'

'I know, and I hate nagging, but just because it's pretty out there don't be lulled into a false sense of security. Looks can be deceptive. You've escaped a nasty situation once—next time you mightn't be so lucky.'

For a second she wasn't sure if he was talking about Jeremy or the bush.

'Take a mobile just to be sure. Please?' he added as she opened her mouth to protest. Grudgingly she nodded. Considering how her previous expedition had turned out, she was hardly in a position to argue.

Ambling through the bush next day, following Ruby's instructions to the letter, Olivia found the clearing easily. Dear Ruby, she had packed her the most the most spectacular lunch and smothered her in factor fifteen sunscreen and the biggest hat. 'Don't youse go getting heatstroke,' she had warned her, waving her off like an anxious mother.

Her weeks in bed had seen spring give way to summer. It was as if the world had been put on fast forward. Pulling back an overgrown bush, she turned into the clearing and Olivia caught her breath in wonder. A flock of rosellas, startled by the intrusion, flew off momentarily, only to return seconds later and adorn a huge coral gum tree, their green and red feathers decorating the old gum spectacularly, like a native Christmas tree.

A tiny stream, its level low from the unforgiving droughts, trickled by and life blossomed around it, the grass lush and green and dotted with flashes of vibrant colour from wild flowers, the bushes laden with berries, a stark contrast to the sunburnt, barren landscapes that had become so familiar. It was a tiny slice of heaven, and just the place to do some serious thinking.

Hungry from her walk, Olivia tucked into her sandwiches. Gradually the birds, which at first had eyed her so suspiciously, gave in to temptation and tentatively approached the crumbs she threw. Surrounded by beauty, she lay back on the grass, closing her eyes against the bright afternoon sun. Now her mind didn't turn automatically to Jeremy. Instead, it was Clem that filled her senses.

She wrestled with her thoughts, trying to fathom what on earth had happened. It was a question she had been trying to avoid. Clem. Sure, she knew patients often mistook their feeling of gratitude for something else. Was that what had happened to her?

Perhaps it was because he had been there for her and could empathise. He understood where she was coming from, knew how lonely the world felt when you came into an empty house at the end of a hard day. He rolled over in bed at night to reach for Kathy the way she had for Jeremy, only to be confronted by a cold, empty space. He, too, had suffered loss, and one far greater than hers.

But then again he had Charlotte. And that hurt. It hurt far more than she liked to admit, and it had nothing to do with how much she didn't like the woman. Just the thought of him with Charlotte made her stomach churn. Had she felt that with Jeremy and Lydia?

Just a few weeks ago she would have given anything to have had Jeremy begging her to come back. She was flattered by his attentions, of course. Proud of him for making consultant as well. After all, he had worked hard enough for the promotion. But what of his proposal? Wouldn't he now expect her to play the part of the consultant's wife—intimate dinner parties, the tennis-club set? Wouldn't he be even more insistent she give up work, with the incentive of a baby and his promise to be faithful if she complied?

All these things she would have done without question and, no doubt, enjoyed, but his infidelity had not only torn apart their relationship, it had forced her to examine herself. She did deserve better. Of course she was pleased that he hadn't just written them off and their engagement hadn't been a total farce. But what was it that Clem had said? That love should make you happy, content and secure. Jeremy had taken all those things from her. At the moment she didn't know what love felt like. The tears had dried up weeks ago and been replaced by a kind of numbness, a hardness that was alien to her.

Packing up her backpack, she emptied the last of the crumbs onto the grass, grateful to Ruby and Clem for letting her in on such a magical place.

Though Olivia had dreaded it, Christmas in Kirrijong turned out to be the happiest she had spent in Australia.

'I didn't know Jeremy was a horticulturalist,' Clem quipped when he arrived on Christmas morning and saw the red roses which had duly arrived the day before.

'What do you mean?'

'Well, his knowledge of flowers is truly amazing! Yellow and then red roses—how exciting! Good God, Livvy, did you really spend five years with him?'

And for the first time she didn't try to defend Jeremy. Instead, she merely laughed as the flyscreen opened and Ruby and Dougie barged in.

'Happy Christmas!' Ruby gathered her into a bear hug while Dougie struggled in with trays of food.

'Happy Christmas!' Olivia laughed, and it really was.

Ruby had embroidered some cushions and Olivia stared in wonder at the tiny delicate stitching, amazed that she had gone to so much effort. Ruby in turn shrieked with delight when she opened her chocolates and smellies.

'My favourites, Livvy. How did you know?'

'You bought them, remember?' Olivia replied warmly, as Ruby yet again enveloped her in a hug.

Clem bought her a compass and a pack of flares, which raised a few laughs, and a huge bottle of her favourite perfume. 'I saw your supplies were getting low,' he said gruffly. He caught her eye and they shared a tiny smile when he opened the jumper Ruby had bought on Olivia's behalf—garish red and green diamonds emblazoned the front.

'Livvy said for me to get youse a pen but I reckoned that you needed a couple more jumpers for those night calls,' Ruby explained with a beaming smile.

They had a barbie in the garden and much later, when they'd settled down to play Monopoly, all cheating shamelessly, Jeremy's inevitable phone call felt to Olivia more like an intrusion than a welcome diversion.

Finally, when the day had ended and Olivia had fallen exhausted but contented into bed, the only thing that had been missing, she reflected, had been mistletoe.

CHAPTER SIX

'THERE is absolutely no need for this. I'm perfectly well. I just want to go back to work.'

'Livvy, do I really need to remind you that you've had glandular fever? I need to examine you thoroughly before I even consider letting you return,' Clem replied, exasperated.

'Well, I'd rather you didn't.' The words came out too harshly, and instantly Olivia regretted her tone. But better that than let him know how she felt. How could she even begin to explain to this impossibly difficult man, who thought she was completely hung up on Jeremy, that her dreams were, in fact, constantly of him, and there was nothing remotely decent about them? It was as if her mind, jaded from self-control and reasoning by day, by night surfaced and took flight, visiting territories alien and uncharted but full of illicit promise.

She could hardly let him examine her. Apart from everything else she was painfully aware of her body. Never voluptuous, the glandular fever had managed to obliterate most of the few curves she'd possessed. Clem might have already seen her at her absolute worst, but she still had some pride. There was no way she was going to let him see her emaciated body.

Running his fingers through his shock of jet hair, Clem threw his pen down on the desk. 'Livvy, you're impossible but, of course, my opinion doesn't count.' He sighed and looked at her pleadingly but she wouldn't relent. 'Obviously I can't force you to let me examine you, but I can refuse to let you back to work till it's documented you're medically fit.'

Olivia frowned. That was something she hadn't considered.

'Look, old Dr Humphreys is coming to town on Tuesday for a consultation. He still has a few old faithfuls that he visits and I'm sure he'd be happy to see you. In the meantime, if you trust me enough, will you let me take your blood? We can at least check your liver function and if that's normal and Dr Humphreys agrees, you can start work again. Very part time, mind you,' he added sharply, ignoring her eager nodding. 'And at the slightest sign you're overdoing it I'll sign you off for a month, and don't think I won't.'

'Fine. And, no, I won't overdo it.'

Rolling up her sleeve, he picked up her arm, frowning slightly in concern. She had gone from being slender to downright skinny. His long fingers traced a vein, then gently he flicked her almost translucent skin to bring the vein to the surface. His dark curls fell over his forehead and Olivia noticed the tiny lines around his eyes as he squinted, concentrating.

She resisted a sudden urge to run her free hand through his hair. She closed her eyes, but he filled her senses. She could smell his aftershave, hear his regular breathing, feel his body close to her. If she fainted now, at least she could blame it on the needle, she thought, for a brief moment revelling in his closeness. Charlotte, Charlotte, Charlotte, she chanted to herself. It was a mantra she found herself repeating at the most inappropriate moments, like now. This really had to stop.

Clem coughed gruffly. Labelling the bottles, he spoke with his back to her. 'You need to put on some serious weight. I'm going to prescribe you a supplement meal drink. I want you to take it three times a day on top of

your regular meals. I'm also going to order an iron screen.
I suspect you're anaemic.'

He turned around and suddenly he wasn't the doctor any
more. 'You need to look after yourself, Livvy. I mean really
look after yourself and not expect too much. This really
isn't the time to be trying to sort things out with Jeremy.
You need a bit of peace. If he puts too much pressure on
just tell him to back off. Don't play games with your
health.'

Touched by his concern and confused by her feelings,
so scared he might read the desire in her eyes, she purposefully rolled down her sleeve and nodded.

'Don't worry, I'll be fine.' It was safer to dismiss him.

Old Dr Humphreys took her blood pressure and listened to
her chest. He must be well over seventy, Olivia thought,
and had the concentration span of a two-year-old.

'Well, Dr Clemson was right. You are seriously under-
weight. How are you feeling?'

'I'm fine,' Olivia replied with more conviction than she
felt. 'I'm just horribly bored and desperate to get back to
work.'

'I don't know, you young sheilas, always wanting to
work. Well, if youse feel well enough I can't see why not.
But any worries, I want you to come straight back.' With
shaking hands he went through her notes. 'You're a tad
anaemic but the supplement will correct that. Your liver
function's normal now, which is good. I'll just take a look
at your stomach.' The telephone interrupted him. 'No, Dr
Clemson will want those results, Betty. No worries, then.'
He replaced the receiver. 'Now, where were we? That's
right, I was about to look at your throat.'

Olivia didn't bother to correct him. Instead, she obediently opened her mouth as he gave her throat a cursory

glance. He really was losing the plot. Just the sort of doctor Jermey had been worried about.

'Well, everything seems in order. I'll arrange another blood test in a month's time to check your iron levels. In the meantime, just take things slowly.'

'I will. Thank you.'

'No worries.'

Leaving the surgery, she walked slap-bang into Clem.

'Everything all right?' he asked.

'Everything's fine. I'll be back at work tomorrow.'

'Why not take the rest of the week off? Start after the weekend. We'll manage.'

'Dr Humphreys said I could start straight back, there really isn't anything to worry about. I'll just do mornings, like we agreed.' Determined to resist his attempts to keep her at home, her voice became more insistent.

'He examined you properly?' Clem demanded, refusing to budge.

Olivia evaded the question. 'Clem, please, you're carrying on like a headless chook.' She darted around him and out of the door. Stopping briefly, she smiled reassuringly. 'I'll see you in the morning.'

For all her efforts to get there, the exhilaration of being back at work soon wore off. If she had been expecting a welcoming committee, or at the very least to be eased into things, she couldn't have been more mistaken. Though the patients were delighted to see her and genuinely concerned about her health, they still wanted to be seen quickly. Clem was at his bloodiest, constantly snapping and downright rude at times, and though Olivia managed to escape most of his wrath, he certainly didn't seem intent on making her first day pleasant.

Olivia spent the afternoon in bed, not waking till the evening, amazed at how exhausted a few hours in the surgery had left her. For a moment she lay there, thinking about Clem. He really was the most complicated man. One moment he was gentle and caring, but he could change like the wind. Part of her was furious at him for treating her poorly on her first day back, while on the other hand she couldn't help but be concerned about his erratic behaviour. These weren't the childish tantrums Jeremy was so good at throwing. Clem's moods seemed to run far deeper. He was a good man, you could just tell. Time and again she had marvelled at his compassion. He never took the easy route to lighten his load.

She thought of baby Moffatt. It would have taken far less effort to have simply called an ambulance and had the baby admitted, and in these days of liability, safer, too. Instead, he had thought of the parents, the strain it would have placed on them, the distance that would have separated them from their newborn and had taken it all on himself. That wasn't the cool, distant man she had seen this morning.

Kathy's death was obviously still affecting him deeply. There was room for compassion and understanding. She hoped Charlotte had what it took to reach him.

Though not hungry, Olivia forced herself to cook some supper and listlessly ate it, knowing she desperately needed to put on some weight. Her clothes were all falling off her and, though never busty, what little she had seemed to be receding at the rate of knots. Taking the revolting meal supplement through to the lounge, Olivia flopped in front of the television and flicked through the channels. There was a good film just starting, a real weepy. Just what she needed. It would do her good to have a real cry over someone else's awful love life.

Just as the film climaxed the doorbell rang. Olivia was in floods of tears, of course. 'Damn.' She went to press the pause button and then remembered it wasn't a video she was watching. Oh, well, she had seen it before and knew it had a happy ending. If only real life was so easy.

There, standing in the doorway was Clem. 'I needed to see you to explain. Your first day back and I behaved appallingly. I've made you cry again after I promised I wouldn't.' He looked completely exhausted and, Olivia guessed rightly, slightly inebriated.

'You didn't make me cry. I was watching a film,' she stated firmly. 'And anyway you didn't promise, you just said you'd try not to. Sit down.' She gestured to the sofa. 'I'll get us some coffee.'

Clem did as he was told but as she turned and headed for the kitchen he reached for her hand, pulling her back to face him. 'I didn't come here for coffee, Livvy. I came to talk. I know I've had a bit too much to drink, and for that I apologise, but I know what I'm saying.' He let go of her hand and for a second she stood there, not sure what to do, uncertain what she might hear, her hand tingling from his touch.

'And what is it you're saying, Clem?' she asked finally. He looked up, his eyes filled with despair and something else she couldn't interpret.

'That I'm worried about you, Livvy, and I don't think Jeremy's very good for you.'

'Well, that's really not for you to decide. But if it makes you feel any better, I had rather worked that one out for myself.'

'Good. You deserve better, like what I had with Kathy. She died two years ago today.'

Putting his face in his hands, Olivia watched, mortified, as a tear slid between his fingers. 'Oh, I didn't realise. I'm so sorry.' So that was what this was all about. His black mood and now this drinking to blot out the pain. She could feel his grief, sense his utter loss. Taking a couple of deep breaths, he composed himself and leant back in the chair, his fingers fiddling aimlessly with the heavy gold band on his wedding ring finger, the pain etched in his strong features so intense it made her want to weep with him.

'I'm so confused. Part of me just wants to lie down with her, but the other part wants to get on with my life. I'm so torn, Livvy.'

Olivia resisted the urge to put her arms around his shoulders and simply cry with him. Maybe it would help but she couldn't be sure.

'I know she would want me to pick up the pieces,' Clem continued. 'She told me so herself. We talked about it once and she said it would break her heart if she thought I was destined to a life of grief and pain alone. I said all the right things, of course. That I'd be all right and she didn't have to worry, but I never thought it would really happen and definitely not so soon. I didn't think I was ready to move on. I certainly wasn't looking for another relationship, then before I knew it...' He was rambling now, but she let him talk without interruption. Better out than in. 'I just feel so damn guilty, and I took it out on everyone, including you. I didn't mean to be so rude. It was just easier today of all days. It's not the day to be making progress.'

Olivia shrugged. 'Perhaps it is. Maybe by talking, by letting things out, you've taken a step in the right direction.'

'I guess so. I've been dreading today and it lived up to my worse expectations. I was thinking about you, and I couldn't bear how I'd behaved, how I'd treated you on your first day back, so I came over to try to explain.'

Her heart went out to him. In the depth of his grief he still had taken the time to come over to apologise and explain his actions. Taking a deep breath, Olivia followed her instincts, battling with her usual reserve. She went over, sitting beside him on the couch. This time she didn't hold back, this time she knew how to respond, and she tenderly put her arms around him as he poured his heart out.

'I just don't know if I'm ready to start again. Part of me is so lonely and it would feel so good to be loved and held, yet part of me says it would be unfaithful to Kathy.'

'Has there been anyone else since Kathy?'' she asked gently. For a moment he didn't answer and she held her breath, terrified she might have intruded too far and equally scared of his answer.

'What do you think?' he answered slowly.

For a moment she sat there quite still. It was a silly question after all. Six feet three, every inch a man. As if he wasn't sleeping with Charlotte. What man wouldn't? So here he was on the anniversary of his wife's death, beating himself up because he'd met someone else. She wanted to scream that Charlotte wasn't good enough, what on earth was he doing with her? But knew she would be speaking out of jealousy. Clem needed a far more objective opinion and, for whatever reason, he had come to her for it.

'Just because you're moving on with your life, it doesn't mean you love Kathy any less. Maybe the time for grieving is over. That doesn't mean you have to forget Kathy. There's enough room in your heart for someone else. Falling in love again doesn't have to detract from the love you shared, and in time you'll work it out.'

She felt him relax against her and she longed to bury her face in his dark hair, to kiss away the pain and tears and somehow make everything all right, but it wasn't her place. All she could do was be there for him.

'You can talk to me, Clem. I'm a friend as well as a colleague, and I hope I always will be. You don't have to bottle things up, it's good to get these things out.' Blindly she continued, almost repeating what he had once said to her and praying she didn't put a foot wrong, ignoring the pain that seared through her as she battled with the image of Clem and Charlotte together in bed.

Feeling his shoulders tense beneath her arm, she knew she must have said the wrong thing.

'You still don't get it, do you?' He read the confusion in her eyes. Shrugging her off, she knew she had lost him. 'Perhaps I will have that coffee after all,' he said flatly. The moment was gone.

Waiting for the kettle to boil, Olivia tried to make sense of the jumbled emotions that coursed through her, and yet despite the confusion her thoughts were amazingly lucid.

Had she fallen in love with Clem? Was it possible to love someone you knew so little about? Sure, she knew Clem was a widower and a kind and caring doctor, and undoubtedly over recent weeks he had become a good friend. But they had never had a relationship, never shared any intimacies bar one kiss, and as intoxicating as it had been to her, it didn't add up to much in the scheme of things.

Yet didn't this man fill her dreams and stir her emotions in a way she had never thought possible? Weren't her feelings amplified around him—a smile, a laugh, a tear, a sob when he was around? Why, he just had to look at her the wrong way and her temper, so usually well in check, would bubble to the surface. With just the faintest brush of his lips she had felt giddy with longing. If Charlotte hadn't paged him that night....

Charlotte! Just thinking her name brought Olivia to her senses. She had no right to even be entertaining such thoughts. And anyway Clem was in the lounge, grieving for Kathy. Even if she could somehow wave a magic wand and make Charlotte disappear, she still had to face the fact that he deeply loved Kathy and always would. Beautiful, forever young Kathy, whose only sin had been to die too soon. How could she ever live up to that?

Carrying the drinks through, she saw Clem sprawled out on the sofa sound asleep. Taking a doona from the blanket box and a pillow from her bed, she tucked them in around him as gently as Clem had done for her countless times during her illness. For a moment she gazed at him, taking in the dark eyelashes fanning his cheeks, his beautiful full lips slightly apart. Lucky, lucky Charlotte. The urge to touch him was irresistible. Tiptoeing forward, she leant over him and gently kissed him on the forehead.

'Goodnight, Clem. Sleep well,' she murmured softly.

He stirred slightly as she crept out. Flicking off the lamp she made her way the short distance to her own room and lay on the bed, concentrating on keeping her breathing even, unable to relax, so conscious of Clem asleep nearby and so scared of what the future held.

It seemed she had only just drifted off when she heard the front door close. Climbing out of bed, she padded through to the lounge. The doona and pillow were now neatly folded on the sofa. Wandering through to the kitchen to make a coffee, Olivia saw a note from Clem on the table. She didn't read it straight away, but forced herself to wait until she was back in bed with a coffee by her side. With a trembling hand she unfolded the paper, wondering what he would have to say in the cold light of day.

'Thanks for listening last night, though I can't recall much of what was said. I don't make a habit of getting drunk and crashing on young women's sofas. (Not recently anyway.) I really think we need to talk.
Clem
P.S. You really ought to keep some aspirin in the house.

Olivia laughed at the last line and then reread the note. Whatever did he want to talk about? He had said it all last night. Clem had needed a friend and confidante and she had been there. Despite his popularity, Clem, Olivia realised, had no one he could really talk to. You couldn't imagine Charlotte talking about anyone but herself for more than five minutes, and at the end of the day, despite their affection for him, every one of Clem's local friends was also his patient.

Olivia realised how lucky she was for, although they were on the other side of the world, her parents were always there when she needed them, if only on the other end of the telephone. Clem's family consisted of his brother, and from what Olivia had heard Joshua wasn't exactly family-orientated. If anyone had had an excuse for drinking too much, Clem had had one last night.

CHAPTER SEVEN

'Could I get James another drink of water, please?'

'I'm a receptionist, not a waitress,' Betty muttered to Olivia. 'That's the third drink they've asked for. You'd think she'd have given him breakfast before they came.'

'It might be nerves. He's not waiting for me to take his blood, is he?' Olivia enquired, looking over at the woman sitting anxiously with her young son.

'No, he's waiting to see Clem. They haven't even got an appointment. I warned Anne that they'll have to wait ages to be seen and now she's making me suffer, like it's my fault. I've enough work to be going on with, without providing a running buffet.'

Her whining voice seemed particularly grating this morning. Olivia shot her a withering look. 'It's not as if you're rushed off your feet. Clem hasn't even arrived yet,' she pointed out.

'Well, I'm going to ring him if he doesn't come soon. I'm fed up with the patients moaning at me about how long they have to wait, yet as soon as they're speaking to Clem it's all sweetness and light.'

For once Clem was late in. Not that Olivia needed him to start her day as there was an endless queue of patients waiting for various tests and dressings. She couldn't help but feel sorry for Clem when he arrived. The waiting room was packed and, given the fact he had spent a night fully clothed on her sofa, he couldn't be feeling his best. She couldn't be sure, but Olivia thought she caught the faintest hint of a blush on his deadpan face as he bade her good morning.

Betty was at her most irritating, trying to hurry Olivia along and juggle her list. 'Mrs Addy has been waiting an hour for her blood test. Why are you seeing James Gardner first? He's not even on your list.'

'Because he doesn't look at all well,' Olivia replied sharply, leading him through to the treatment room. That was an understatement. He looked as if he was about to pass out. Even if he just lay in a screened-off area till Clem could take a look, at least she could do some obs and keep an eye on him.

Scanning his notes, she saw that James was nearly ten years old and, apart from the usual childhood illnesses, he had always been healthy. Carefully she checked his heart rate and respirations, which were slightly raised. Popping a thermometer into his mouth, she noted that his lips were cracked and he looked dehydrated. 'You're not feeling the best, are you, mate?' She smiled sympathetically at the boy. 'I'll just ask your mum what's been going on.'

He nodded his agreement.

'Mrs Gardner.'

'Please, call me Anne.'

'Anne, how long has James been unwell?'

'A few days. I thought it was some twenty-four-hour bug he'd picked up from school so I kept him home, but he's getting worse. He's at the toilet every five minutes, though I'm not surprised—he's drinking heaps. I think he might have a urine infection. He didn't want to come to the doctor, they get embarrassed at this age.'

Olivia nodded. 'I know. But you're obviously unwell, James. The doctor's used to this sort of thing. It's best to get it sorted.'

'There's something wrong, I know it. I'd never normally turn up without an appointment. Betty was really put out, but I could hardly wake him this morning, Sister.'

'Don't worry about Betty. You're his mum, you know if

your child is sick. I'll just take his blood pressure and I'll get Clem to come and have a look.' And then I'll strangle Betty, Olivia fumed to herself.

'I don't want to jump the queue. I don't mind waiting,' Anne said.

'He needs to be seen,' Olivia said matter-of-factly.

James's temperature was normal but Anne was right—there was definitely something going on. Wrapping the cuff around his arm, Olivia leant forward, subtly smelling his breath as she took his blood pressure. With dismay she knew her hunch was right—there was no mistaking the classic pear drop scent, all too familiar from her years in Casualty.

'James, your blood pressure's fine, but if you don't mind I'm just going to do a finger-prick test to check your blood sugar. It will only sting for a second.'

'No worries,' he mumbled, hardly flinching as she pricked his finger. His mother watched anxiously.

His blood sugar was so high she couldn't get an accurate reading. It was a textbook case of diabetes—the unquenchable thirst, the acetone smell on his breath.

'I'll just go and get Clem.'

Betty was really flustered now. 'Mrs Addy was the first patient here,' she said. Mrs Addy was also her sister-in-law, Betty failed to mention, and obviously expected a few favours.

'I'll see her when I can, not when you tell me,' Olivia snapped, furious with Betty for making the Gardners' wretched morning just that bit harder for them. 'Is Clem with a patient?'

Betty, realising she might have overstepped the mark, adopted a more professional manner. 'He's just finished with a patient, but he's on the phone. I'll buzz him and let him know you're coming.'

Such was her concern for young James, Olivia actually

forgot to be embarrassed as she walked into his office, but when she realised Clem was on the phone to Charlotte, nerves caught up with her.

'Look, Charlotte, I'm really snowed under.' He motioned to Olivia to sit as he attempted to finish the conversation. 'I'll see you tomorrow when you get here, and don't worry.' Clem rolled his eyes upwards. 'OK, we'll sort that out later. Drive carefully.' Putting down the phone, he gave her a rueful smile. 'I bet you're feeling a lot better than I am this morning.'

'Probably,' she replied lightly, 'but I've got a James Gardner in the treatment room who, I can guarantee, is feeling worse than you. He was waiting with his mum to see you, but he looked so awful I took him in the treatment room to do some obs. I noticed his breath smelt of ketones so I took a blood glucose. It's off the scale.' Clem stood up. 'He actually doesn't look too bad, considering just how high his glucose is.'

'What have you told him?'

'Nothing yet. Anne knows he's sick but she seems to think it's a urinary infection. It's going to be a shock.'

'Poor kid.' He shook his head. 'Good pick-up, Livvy.'

For some reason she found it impossible to take a compliment from him. 'Hardly. You'd have to be blind to miss it,' she replied, embarrassed but flattered.

He caught her arm in the doorway. 'Many would have let him wait. You're good at your job, Livvy, good at what you do. Don't sell yourself short.'

Yet again Olivia marvelled at his tact and skill with patients. After examining James thoroughly, he somehow managed to sum up the gravity of the situation to James and Anne without alarming them.

'You definitely need to go to hospital, James. Your sugar's very high and you'll need some treatment to get it back to normal. The medicine you need is called insulin, and for now it has to be given in a drip.' He gave him a wide smile. 'You're going to have to wait for that ride in the helicopter, mate. You're sick, but not that sick. We'll get the treatment started and then Livvy and I will look after you till the ambulance gets here. How does that sound?'

James nodded. He was too sick to care, and hardly batted an eyelid when Clem inserted the intravenous cannula. Anne seemed to feel the pain for him.

'He'll be all right, won't he?' she asked, trying desperately to stay calm in front of her son.

Clem beckoned her over to the door out of earshot of James, who lay half-asleep on the trolley. 'He's going to be fine. But he's going to have a lot to deal with. Once he's stabilised he's still going to need the insulin. Do you know about diabetes?'

Anne nodded. 'My sister has it. She has to inject herself twice a day. Will it be the same for him?' she asked, fighting back the tears.

'Yes,' he replied, and Olivia knew that the truth, however brutal, sometimes just needed to be told. 'And it will be hard for James to accept that,' Clem continued, gently but firmly. 'We're going to have to help him realise his diabetes is completely manageable, and that it isn't going to stop him leading a full and active life. He will be all right,' he reiterated. 'Once in hospital, as well as treating him medically, they'll educate James and you all about diabetes. By the time he comes home he'll be telling me what to do—and I'm only half joking.'

Anne managed a wobbly smile and then started to cry. 'I'm sorry. It's just such a shock.'

'Of course it is,' Clem said gently. 'The ambulance will be despatched from the base hospital—it will probably take a couple of hours. Would you like me to ring Andy for you?'

Anne shook her head. 'No, I'll ring and tell him myself, but thanks, Clem.'

Clem had a word with Betty, now the picture of concern, and she ushered Anne into Clem's room so she could speak to her husband in private.

Walking over to Olivia, he gave a wry smile. 'She thanked me, can you believe it? Hell, this is a lousy job sometimes.'

Olivia didn't say anything—she knew he was right.

'I think we'd better start an insulin infusion here. Ideally I'd like to wait till he's admitted, but as that's going to take a while I think it would be safer to get things under way. Are you happy with that?'

Olivia nodded her consent and set about preparing the insulin in a saline and potassium infusion. In no time everything was under control and Olivia carried on with her other duties while keeping a watchful eye on James. The ambulance took nearly two hours to arrive but James's condition didn't deteriorate—in fact, his sugar started to come down. However, he still needed close observation and it was a relief when he was safely on his way.

Olivia enjoyed being busy. It was actually nice in some ways to have such an acute patient. It was like being back in Casualty, but the morning completely exhausted her. She didn't need to be asked twice when Clem popped his head around the door on his way out to home visits to suggest she leave all the paperwork till later and go home and rest. 'There's nothing here that can't wait. You try and have a sleep this afternoon. Don't forget how sick you've been.'

'I won't.' As he went to leave, Olivia knew she couldn't just let him walk away without checking he was all right. 'Clem.'

He turned in the doorway.

'How do you feel?'

He shrugged slightly. 'Nothing that a good night's sleep won't fix,' he answered, too casually.

Olivia nodded, not wanting to push. 'You know where I am.'

Clem nodded. 'I've really got to go. I've got a house call right on the outskirts and it's going to take me ages to get there. But thanks.' He smiled. 'For everything.'

Boosted by their conversation, Olivia decided to at least sort out the paperwork. Some she could take home and maybe do this evening. Betty was bustling about, straightening magazines, determined to stretch her hours so she could claim overtime. The phone ringing finally gave her something to do, yet she still managed to complain about it. Olivia collected up the last of the files and flung her bag over her shoulder.

'A cup of tea, Sister? Clem just rang. He forgot some tablets so he's on his way back. I thought I'd make a brew.'

Olivia suppressed a smile, thinking of Clem's revelation about hating tea. 'No, thanks, Betty. I'm finished here. I'm going home.'

Even before she heard the frantic banging on the surgery door, some sixth sense told her the sound of running footsteps on the drive were those of someone in real trouble. With lightning speed she ran to the door and undid the bolt. A young man who couldn't have been more than twenty stood there, breathless, his face etched with fear and panic. 'She's in the car. She's having it.'

And Olivia knew this was no first-time father getting over-excited.

Betty let out a moan of horror when she saw the man. 'Young Lorna, but she isn't due for months yet.'

Grabbing a wheelchair from the entrance, Olivia raced over to the car. 'Lorna Hall, is it?'

He nodded. She remembered Lorna from the antenatal

clinic. She hadn't seen her for a while but she'd be no more than twenty-six weeks gestation.

'She's in agony, the contractions just keep coming.'

She could hear the terror in his voice. 'What's your name?'

'Pete.'

'OK, Pete, you just stay calm and follow my instructions.' Olivia steeled herself. Taking a deep breath, she opened the car door. Keeping her voice as calm as possible, she greeted the terrified Lorna and briefly examined her. The forewaters were bulging and Olivia knew that if her waters broke the baby could be here in seconds.

'I want to push,' she screamed.

'Not yet,' Olivia said firmly. That was the last thing she wanted her to do. If she could just get them inside the surgery, at least there she had some equipment. It looked as if this baby was going to need all the help available. She looked anxiously over her shoulder. Where the heck was Betty when you needed her? Then she steadied herself. Betty would do the right thing, of course. She'd be ringing Clem to tell him to step on it.

With Pete's help they managed to get Lorna into the wheelchair and rushed her inside. She was trembling all over, her toes curled with the effort of not pushing. Inside, Betty and Pete lifted Lorna onto the examination couch while Olivia hastily pulled on some gloves. She made a mental note to later praise Betty for her efforts. Not only had she rung Clem but also Iris Sawyer and she had managed to plug in the resuscitation cot and open the emergency delivery pack. Lorna started to scream in earnest and Olivia knew this was it. This baby was coming, ready or not.

'I've got to push.'

'OK, Lorna, just hold on a moment longer.' She turned to Betty.

'Go and get the Doppler. It's on my desk.' Betty shook her head. 'Doppler?' Olivia could hear the apprehension in her voice and knew she had confused her. 'I don't know what you mean.'

Olivia forced a reassuring smile. She knew she had to keep Betty calm. 'I use it in my antenatal clinics. It's like a microphone attached to a speaker, to hear the baby's heart,' she said, and mercifully the penny dropped.

'Oh, yes.' Betty rushed off and returned seconds later.

Olivia squirted some jelly on Lorna's abdomen and, having felt the baby's position, she placed the Doppler and listened for the heartbeat, the microphone magnifying the sound for all to hear. Everyone relaxed for a second as a heartbeat was picked up—everyone, that was, but Olivia. The heartbeat was dangerously slow and dipping lower during the contraction. The baby was in foetal distress and the low rate told Olivia there wasn't much time. This baby needed to be born and quickly.

Slipping an oxygen mask over the young woman's face, Olivia explained in reassuring tones what she was about to do. 'You breathe normally. The extra oxygen you're getting will help your baby. I'm going to break your waters. It won't hurt, I promise. You'll just feel a gush.'

Deftly she grabbed the tiny hook-like instrument and ruptured the membranes, knowing this would expedite the birth. The liquor was stained with meconium, which was normally the baby's first bowel movement after birth. The fact the baby had passed this was another sign it was in danger, and if it were to inhale the meconium at birth it could run into all sorts of problems.

'I've got to push,' Lorna screamed.

Betty took Peter's arm. 'You wait outside, pet.' She led him away.

'No, Betty, Pete should be here.'

Betty turned and looked imploringly at Olivia.

'Lorna needs him,' Olivia said firmly, while nodding in understanding. Things certainly didn't look good, but this was his child and he had every right to be there. Apart from anything else, she needed every pair of hands available. 'Pete, hold Lorna's hand, and get her to follow my instructions.'

He did as he was told and much more, guiding and coaxing his terrified wife, drawing on an inner reserve that people somehow found in times of desperation.

Listening to the baby's heartbeat, this time Olivia knew there was no chance of Clem making it back in time. If she didn't get the baby out it would be too late. For a second she felt panic rise in her. But only for a second. It was as if she were on autopilot, in some ghastly, complicated birth video that she had watched in her midwifery training—except this time she was the co-star and poor Lorna the heroine. She'd broken the waters. Lorna had to do the rest.

For a second Olivia eyed the shiny stainless-steel forceps and thought about what Clem would do if he were here. He would probably use them. After all, if this baby wasn't born quickly it didn't stand a chance. But she didn't have the qualifications or experience, and in the wrong hands they could be lethal. Resolutely she looked away. It was up to her and Mother Nature. Despite the other people in the room, never had she felt more alone.

'Lorna, when the next contraction comes I want you to push as hard as you can, right into your bottom. I want you to really push hard,' Olivia repeated. 'Just concentrate on that, and don't stop till I tell you.'

Lorna nodded, then the pain took over. 'It's coming again.'

'Right, push. Come on, push hard.' They all encouraged her. Pete, oblivious of his wife's nails digging into his forearm, coaxed her, demanding that she keep on pushing.

'I can't,' Lorna screamed.

'Yes, you can, you're doing marvellously. Keep pushing. The harder you push the sooner your baby will be here,' Olivia encouraged, as the tiny head emerged. She swiftly suctioned the tiny nose and mouth so the baby wouldn't inhale the meconium when it took its first breath. Deftly she felt around the baby's neck and with dismay she realised the umbilical cord was wrapped around it.

'Don't push,' Olivia said firmly.

'But I have to.'

'No, Lorna. You mustn't. I want you to blow instead, like you're blowing out a candle. Don't push,' she reiterated, for if Lorna pushed now the cord would tighten around the baby's neck. Pete took over, telling his wife exactly what to do, leaving Olivia free to deal with the baby. Swiftly she grabbed the clamps and clamped and cut the cord. The infant's colour was ghastly.

'Lorna, I want you to push now.'

Lorna flailed exhausted, against the pillow. 'I don't need to, I'm not having a contraction,' she said faintly.

'You still have to push—your baby needs to be born.' For a split second their eyes locked and it was all it took to relay the urgency of the message. With her new maternal instinct Lorna somehow found the strength to push. Her young face purple from the exertion and pain, she pushed for all she was worth and when it was all too much Pete inspired her to push some more.

Olivia delivered the tiny baby and, leaving Betty and Pete to look after Lorna, she glanced at the clock as she rushed over to the resuscitation cot, the tiny form grey and limp in her hands. Laying him down, she again swiftly suctioned his tiny nose and mouth, and with infinite relief she saw him make the tiniest respiratory effort but his breathing was far too slow and irregular. Using her stethoscope, she listened to his heart, alarmed at its slowness. The baby's extreme bradycardia combined with his minimal respiratory effort meant that he wasn't being anywhere near sufficiently oxygenated, and Olivia was left with no choice but to commence a full resuscitation. With the ambu-bag she gently pushed oxygen into his lungs and massaged the tiny chest with her fingers, counting the compressions in her head as she willed the baby to respond.

'Why isn't it crying? Why isn't my baby crying?' Lorna begged, while Pete tried to reassure his wife.

'Sister's doing all she can. It'll all be all right, Clem's here now.'

Olivia didn't have time to acknowledge Clem's arrival but she had never in her life been so pleased to see anyone. He took over the respirations as she continued to massage the chest.

'What was his one-minute Apgar?' asked Clem, referring to the initial assessment Olivia had made of the baby. A score of three or less indicated a gravely ill infant.

'Two.'

'How long's it been?'

Olivia looked at the clock and for a second she thought it had stopped. Had it really only been three minutes since this tiny little boy had come into the world? It felt like an hour. 'Three minutes. Oh, come on, baby, breathe, please.'

Time seemed to take on no meaning as the world ran in slow motion. The baby's heart rate picked up, which meant she could take over the respirations while Clem, with great skill, managed to insert a line into the umbilical cord and administer lifesaving drugs directly into the baby's system.

Suddenly Olivia felt the faintest resistance in the ambu-bag. She saw his rib cage flutter and rise as his lungs expanded on their own. His flaccid limbs started to move, his tiny fists clenching. He started to cry, not the normal, lusty scream of a healthy newborn but a tiny wail like a mewing kitten. But it was a cry nonetheless, and the tension in the room lifted slightly. He was by no means out of the woods but at least they were heading in the right direction.

Olivia attached him to a multitude of monitors as Clem went off to briefly check on Lorna. Gently Olivia stroked the tiny infant's cheek. He might have got off to a lousy start in life but he did have some luck on his side. His GP was a fully qualified paediatrician after all. Clem was back in a moment.

'How's Lorna?'

'Terrified, of course, but Iris is here and she's very good. They heard him cry and I've briefly told them what's going on. I'll explain more when I know myself. Now, let's see how he's doing.' They looked at the array of monitors. 'What did you make his five-minute Apgar?'

'Seven.'

Clem nodded in agreement. 'Which is a good pick-up.' He listened to the newborn's chest. 'He's struggling and his oxygen saturation's low. Put him in a head box and we'll see if they improve.'

Olivia nodded. The baby was using his accessory muscles and grunting with each exhausting breath. He looked like a tiny washed-up frog.

'Betty's ringing the emergency transfer team, but it will be a while till they can get here.'

'Where will he be going?' Olivia asked as she set up the equipment that would enable the baby to receive a higher concentration of oxygen.

'Melbourne or Sydney, wherever there's an intensive care bed.'

Betty appeared and, unable to tear her eyes away from the tiny newborn, relayed her message. 'I've got the emergency transfer team on the line.'

'Thanks, Betty.' Clem nodded to Olivia. 'I'm going to get some much-needed advice from them and then I'll be back, but if there's any change tell Betty to come and get me straight away.'

Olivia nodded without looking up—there really wasn't any time for niceties.

Betty stood there, frozen. 'I've never seen one as small,' she said in a choked voice. 'But he's so perfect.'

One of the monitors was causing Olivia some alarm, and she didn't respond to Betty's comments. The baby's oxygen saturation level, never particularly good, was now starting to fall. She checked the probe attached to his tiny foot and the flow level to the oxygen head box. All the equipment was working perfectly. 'Betty, tell Clem his oxygen saturation has dropped to 80 per cent and is falling.'

'Eighty per cent,' Betty repeated, and rushed off.

Clem returned within a moment. 'The transfer team is mobilising—they've got a bed for him in Sydney. We were just debating whether to intubate yet or wait for them to arrive, but as his sats are falling they said to go ahead now.' A tiny muscle was flickering in his cheek, the only sign that this was causing him any concern. Apart from that detail, he looked as impeccably cool and in control as always. 'Set up an intubation tray, please, Livvy.' He gave her a reassuring smile. 'Don't worry, I did a stint in anaesthetics before I came to practise in the middle of nowhere.'

Olivia smiled in what she hoped was a reassuring manner. Despite Clem's apparent confidence, she knew he must be apprehensive. It was one thing to be competent at emergency anaesthetics, and he would obviously get practice out here, but a baby this tiny was a totally different ball game. Poor Clem. Still, they had no choice.

'Betty, take Pete and Lorna into another room. Stay with them and ask Iris to come in here.' He paused for a moment. 'Actually, you stay here and tell Iris to stay with Lorna. Livvy, move the phone over here. There's an anaesthetist on the line and he's going to talk me through in case I need any help.'

Betty held the receiver to Clem's ear as Olivia assisted Clem with the procedure. Thankfully the intubation went smoothly and in no time the baby was connected to the respirator. Through it all they were guided by the experts in Sydney. Again she realised how well stocked Clem had the surgery. Most of the drugs and equipment that the neonatal doctors recommended they had, and so were able to follow the instructions almost to the letter without having to make do. This baby really was being given every opportunity.

When his condition had stabilised, and on the advice of the transfer team, they wheeled Lorna and Pete in to finally see their baby. Olivia bit hard on her lip, fighting back tears as Lorna, with shaking hands, reached into the portholes and touched her tiny son. Pete held her shoulders as tears streamed down his face.

'It's all right, baby, Mummy's here,' Lorna soothed her son, gazing in wonder at the tiny hands she held, no bigger than her fingernails.

'He looks so tiny,' Pete said in a gruff voice. 'So fragile and helpless.' He stared at the monitors. 'All this equipment?'

'I know the monitors look frightening,' Olivia explained gently, 'but they're all helping him and giving us the information we need. None of them are hurting him.'

'But he was crying before. Why isn't he now? And why has he got that tube down his throat?' Lorna asked shakily.

Clem had already explained what each of the monitors and tubes were for, before he'd bought them to see their son, but obviously in their anguish it had been too much to take in. With infinite gentleness he explained again. 'That tube is helping him to breathe. You're right. He was crying, and he was breathing on his own, which is a very good sign. We chose to do this because his little lungs are too small to cope at the moment and he was getting exhausted. This machine will do the breathing for him and give him a chance to rest.'

'He'll be all right, though? He'll make it, won't he?' Lorna was inconsolable and unfortunately there were no guarantees.

'He's got a long battle ahead of him, but he's going to a great hospital. The emergency transfer team is coming here to get him and I'm constantly in contact with the specialists in Sydney. They'll be here soon. We're doing everything we can.'

'Can I go with him in the helicopter?' Lorna asked.

'That's not up to me, Lorna. The transfer team will have to decide,' Clem answered gently. 'There's not much room on board with all the staff and equipment. It will have to be up to them—they know best.'

Lorna started to cry in earnest, completely overwhelmed. 'He's just so small…'

Clem nodded. 'He's pretty tough, though, and he's made it over the first hurdle. With expert care he'll have the best possible chance.'

Pete cradled his wife in his arms. 'He's got a chance, Lorna. Clem says so. That's enough to be going on with for now. Let's just be grateful for that.'

The wait was interminable but finally the sound of the helicopter heralded the arrival of the emergency team. They wheeled in a huge incubator equipped with everything the baby would need to get him safely to Sydney. Olivia could only stand back and marvel at their skills. They handled the tiny baby so expertly and confidently, attaching him to their equipment, assessing his condition each step of the way.

They were there for well over an hour, ensuring he was completely stable before they transferred him, all the time reassuring his parents. They even took a couple of Polaroid photos, one of the baby and the other of Lorna and Pete next to the incubator, holding their tiny son's hand. Pete's parents arrived as Olivia was helping Lorna, stunned and exhausted, into the helicopter, but there was no time for them to see their newborn grandson. The baby's needs had to take precedence.

'Give these to Pete,' Lorna said in a shaking voice, handing Olivia the Polaroids. 'He can show them the photos.'

Impulsively Olivia reached over and hugged Lorna tightly.

Lorna clung on, grateful for the human touch but completely unaware how out of character this was for Olivia. 'Thank you, Livvy, thank you,' she said tearfully.

As the helicopter left, carrying its precious load, Clem turned to Pete. 'Are your parents going to drive you to Sydney?' Clem asked.

Pete nodded, tears coursing down his cheeks as he gazed at the photos.

'Well, take it steady,' he said, as practical as ever. 'The last thing Lorna needs is for you to be involved in accident. I'll ring the hospital later, see how he's doing.' His voice wavered slightly. 'Chin up, mate.' Clem shook Pete's hand. 'We'll all be thinking of you.'

As they waved off the car, watching it crunch its way down the gravel path to whatever the future held for them, Olivia finally broke down. Clem said nothing, just pulled her into his arms and let her cry. Finally, as the sobs subsided, he lifted her chin to make her look at him. 'Not the ideal first delivery, but you did a fantastic job.'

'If I had just got him out sooner, but the cord—'

'Don't do that to yourself. You did absolutely everything anyone could have done. Any hope he's got is because of you, so don't beat yourself up with what ifs. You gave him a chance.'

Olivia nodded, glad he understood. She knew she couldn't have done anything differently, but she just needed to hear it. His arms still around her, he looked down.

'You look completely done in.'

'It's been an exhausting day.' Olivia wriggled away, suddenly conscious of his embrace. 'Where's Betty?'

'Off to tell the whole town, no doubt. She's a terrible sticky beak.'

Olivia was about to agree, then remembered the wisdom Betty had shown when it had been needed. 'She really helped in there.'

'Why do you think I keep her on? I know she's a lousy receptionist but her heart is in the right place and she does come up trumps when you need her. I'm very choosy about my staff. That's why your predecessors didn't last.'

'Really?' Olivia frowned 'The agency gave the impression they left because...' Her voice trailed off. She could hardly repeat what Miss Lever had said about him.

'Because I was moody and difficult?'

Olivia shuffled uncomfortably. 'Something like that.'

'And is that how you find me?' he enquired.

Olivia thought for a moment.

'Yes,' she answered truthfully. 'Though not in the way I expected. I mean, you're a very good doctor and a wonderful boss...'

'But?'

'But nothing that would make me want to pack up and leave, unless, of course, I didn't want to be here in the first place.'

'Exactly. You've got it in one. A lot of people seem to think they'll come out here for a bit of a holiday and, as you know, it couldn't be further from the truth. At the end of the day, to the people here we're all they've got medically speaking. It's an awesome responsibility.'

'I know, and it terrifies me. I have to remind myself

sometimes that I ran a busy casualty department, and that I'm used to making difficult decisions and I am up to this. But sometimes, like today, I realise that we're alone at the front line. In Casualty there was always someone to confer with, someone's opinion there for the asking. I don't know how you do it. It must get pretty scary sometimes.'

'It does and that's the very reason I only keep good staff. I'd rather struggle on alone than with someone who isn't up to it. Take today. Betty is a receptionist—that's all she's paid for. Sure, I give her a few perks and sometimes I think it's more than she deserves. But just as she's seriously getting on my nerves and I think it's time I put my foot down and had a word, she outshines herself like she did this afternoon. It makes the incessant personal calls and sticky-beaking look rather irrelevant.'

Olivia understood. Betty really had been marvellous.

'So when some young nurse arrives, and straight away asks where the local hotel is, running out the door on the stroke of five and taking the phone off the hook at night, I have no compunction about being as moody and difficult as my reputation allows. You, on the other hand are the complete opposite. We work pretty damn well together.'

Olivia took this all in, touched by his praise but embarrassed as well. 'So why are you still so moody and difficult with me, then?' she teased, shrugging off his compliments.

He didn't answer. Instead, he stared at her for what seemed an eternity. Finally she dragged her eyes away. Clem cleared his throat. 'I don't know about you, but I could do with a stiff drink and I don't fancy fielding questions from concerned locals down at the hotel. Anyway, I want to ring the hospital later see how he's getting on.' He gestured to the private part of the house. 'Will you join me?'

Olivia hesitated, torn. It was certainly tempting to spend the evening with him but, given her feelings, she wasn't sure it was appropriate. But surely a drink with a friend after the afternoon they'd had wasn't unreasonable, and anyway she wanted to be there when he rang the hospital. She looked down at her soiled clothing. 'I'll go home and have a bath and change first. There wasn't exactly time to put on an apron.'

Clem smiled, noticing for the first time the mess she was in. 'Fair enough. I'll wait for you to come over before I ring.'

Olivia nodded. She knew how he felt. Neither wanted to be alone if the news was bad.

CHAPTER EIGHT

UP TO her neck in bubbles, Olivia tortured herself by going over and over the events. Oh, she knew what Clem had said and hoped it was true, but if only she'd .had more experience. Was there *anything* she could have done differently?

Getting out the bath, despite a huge fluffy bathrobe and the warm evening, Olivia couldn't stop shaking. She suddenly felt light-headed. Clutching the bedside table, she sat down on the edge of the bed, waiting for the dizziness to pass. Maybe the bath had been too warm, Olivia reasoned as she relived the birth for the umpteenth time. Perhaps there *had been* something more she could have done, and Clem, knowing how hard she had tried and how upset she was, didn't want to make her feel worse. Of course not, she admonished herself. Clem was a wonderful teacher. If there was anything to be learnt from today he would have told her, no matter how hard it might be to hear. Still, an incessant voice kept nagging, maybe she could have done better.

She dressed slowly, pulling on some denim shorts and a white cotton blouse. A niggling pain in her shoulder made putting on her make-up more of a chore than usual, but without it her complexion was so pale, and Clem would only start nagging about her being back at work. The phone started to ring as she picked up her keys and grabbed a bottle from the fridge. The answering machine could get it. She didn't have to explain where she was going to anyone.

Clem greeted her warmly. 'I was starting to think about calling out the search party again.'

'Am I ever going to live that down?' Olivia grinned, offering the bottle she had brought.

'Not if I have any say in it.' He looked at the bottle 'Champagne. Are we celebrating?'

'To toast my first delivery in Kirrijong.' He caught the flash of tears in her eyes. 'It might not have been as I planned, but he deserves to have his head wet. It's still a miracle.'

'Oh, Livvy.' He swept her into his arms. 'Of course it's a miracle. That little tacker has touched us all—he's a fighter. Come on, we'll have a drink and then we'll ring to see how he's doing.'

He led her through to the lounge and sat her down. It was a room she had her lunch in every day and yet by evening light and without Betty it felt completely different. The heavy drapes were drawn and the gentle lighting illuminated the welcoming warmth and intimacy of this beautiful home. As Clem popped the cork he shot her a wary look. 'Your liver function test was normal?'

'Perfectly.'

'I still wish you'd let me check you. Nothing against Dr Humphreys. He was a fine doctor.'

'Was' being the operative word, Olivia thought, but didn't say anything. 'How's the hospital going?'

'Painfully slowly. That's two patients today who really needed it. Of course, Lorna and the baby would have been transferred anyway, but it would be nice to have an anaesthetist and a few more pairs of hands. Not,' he added, handing her a glass of champagne, 'that we didn't cope admirably, but I'm tired of coping, and constantly being on call makes it impossible to relax. Take yesterday. I had to ask Dr Humphreys weeks in advance to cover for me because I knew I'd need a night to myself, what with Kathy's anniversary and everything. Not that I was planning to get plastered, I hasten to add. That rather took care of itself. I really am sorry.'

'Clem, please, don't apologise. There's really no need and, anyway, you really weren't that bad.' She changed the subject. 'So, when do you think it will be up and running?'

'Another couple of months. I'm going to start advertising for staff.'

'Do you think you'll have much luck?'

Clem looked at her thoughtfully. 'There shouldn't be too much trouble. It's a different kettle of fish, recruiting for a country hospital compared to a GP practice. The incentives will be pretty good and there'll be a lot of experience to be gained. At least they won't have to ship every remotely interesting case off to the base hospital. The serious ones will still go to Melbourne or Sydney, but that's pretty standard.' He paused, as if about to say something.

Olivia waited. He had never formally offered her a job there, and she had just assumed that there would be one. Still, it would be nice to be asked. Clem didn't say anything, just reached over and refilled her glass. He obviously had other things on his mind.

She put her hand over the top of the glass and some champagne trickled through her fingers. 'That's plenty, thanks. I haven't had a drink in ages it will go straight to my head.'

Clem stood up. 'A fine host I am. You haven't eaten dinner, and I'm the one insisting you eat regular meals and fatten up. I'll fix us something now.'

'Please, don't. I'm honestly not hungry.'

He ignored her, of course. 'Just wait there. Put on some music, make yourself comfortable.'

He disappeared into the kitchen and Olivia eyed his music collection. It was far more familiar than the highbrow operas Jeremy pretended to listen to, and at least his stereo system looked user-friendly and Clem actually had cassettes. Jeremy's was all CDs and digital everything. It looked like a flight deck in a Boeing 747.

Settling on a hits mix she smiled as he entered.

'Dinner will be twelve minutes, according to the box.' He picked up the cassette holder Olivia had chosen. 'Now there's a blast from the past.'

'It reminds me of my wild youth.'

Clem raised an eyebrow. 'Really, Sister Morrell?'

'No, but I sometimes wish it had been.'

'Well, you sit there and reminisce about what could have been and I'll ring the hospital.'

Olivia nodded. She had been waiting for him to ring but had been too terrified of what the outcome might be to suggest it herself.

He was back within a few moments. 'He's stable.'

She let out a sigh of relief and Clem continued, 'There's been no major dramas since he left us, all his vital signs are as good as can be expected.'

Olivia digested this, but the question that was eating at her had to be asked. 'What about…?' She hesitated, unable to get the words out.

'Brain damage?' He asked the question for her. 'Livvy, you know it's far too soon to even begin to answer that. It could be weeks, months even, before they know.'

Oh, she knew that, knew all the statistics and that brain injury wasn't always immediately apparent, and she knew that there was still a lot to happen that could influence the outcome, but it wasn't enough. She turned her huge green eyes on him. 'But what do you think, Clem? What's your own opinion?'

Clem put down his glass. He knew she felt guilty, and with absolutely no reason. It was just part of the job. If you cared enough you got involved. 'I think,' he said slowly, 'that the little guy and Lorna and Pete have a struggle on their hands. No baby born at twenty-six weeks gestation sails through. If he comes out of this totally unscathed it will be a miracle. But miracles do happen, we saw that today. His one-minute Apgar was awful, but he was resuscitated very effectively and he picked up quickly—that counts for a lot. He looked in pretty good shape for such a premmie by the time the transfer team got here. I think we can be cautiously optimistic, and confident we did all we could and did it well.

'Hell.' Clem stood up suddenly. 'I forgot about the dinner.'

He returned minutes later with a vast pizza. 'I hope you like them crusty.' He laughed as he cut the pizza into generous slices. They knelt at the coffee-table, eating the pizza from the serving plate. Despite her earlier protests, Olivia realised she was hungry after all and tucked in unashamedly. About to reach for her third slice, she felt Clem staring at her.

'What are you staring at? Have I got something on my face?'

'Relax, I was just thinking how other woman must hate you. No matter what you eat, you never gain an ounce.'

'Nerves,' Olivia quipped. 'I'm just a bundle of them. It's probably just as well my life's in such a mess. The day I'm actually content I'll probably pile on the kilos and end up with hips you could—' Suddenly, and she never knew quite how it happened, Clem put a finger up to her lips and she knew the time for talking had ended.

'Livvy, look at me.'

She sat there quite still as he gently lifted her chin and slowly she raised her eyes to meet his. It was like looking in a mirror, seeing the burning desire she felt reflected in his, and she was finally in no doubt her feelings were reciprocated. Her heart was racing, her breathing speeding up, making her breasts rise and fall rapidly. He hadn't even kissed her yet, but the effect of this handsome, sensual man close up was more intoxicating than any champagne.

Sensing her consent, driven by his own desire, Clem moved his face towards her and teasingly showered her face then her neck with tiny butterfly kisses. Her eyes closed, her lips parted, she drowned in her senses, the bitter tang of his aftershave, the sweetness of his lips on her smooth skin.

Finally his mouth found hers and hungrily he kissed her, desperately forcing her lips apart with his tongue. He tasted of champagne and decadence and danger. She could feel the rising current that surged between them, hear their hearts beating in unison, and she revelled in it.

The distance from the living room to the bedroom was quickly negotiated and gently he laid her on the bed, all the time kissing her as if he couldn't bear to let her go. And she didn't want him to. Her ardour rising with each gasping breath, she could feel his hard, muscular body pushing against her slender frame. Instinctively she arched her body towards him, inflaming the fire that burnt between them. Expertly he undid her blouse and gasped as his searching hands encountered the gentle swell of her ripe breasts, a delicious contrast to her slender body.

With a gentle moan he buried his head into the velvet softness of her bosom, his tongue enticing her hardening nipples. One tender hand stroked her neck, while the other slowly, deliberately moved down, and Olivia knew she wanted him to go on, ached for him to go further.

'Are you sure, Livvy?' His eyes locked with hers and she nodded her consent.

'I'm sure,' she murmured, her voice not wavering as she gazed into his eyes. 'What about…?'

Gesturing to the *en suite,* he went to climb out of bed, but she gently pulled him back. 'No. I'll go.'

She darted into the bathroom, grateful for the chance to

gather her thoughts. She wanted that brief moment. Gazing in the mirror at her flushed cheeks and bright eyes, her lips red and full from the weight of his kiss, she knew that she had never been surer of anything in her life. Rummaging through his cabinet, she found the tiny foil packages and, ever the nurse, checked the expiry date on the back. A gurgle of laughter escaped from her lips as she realised that here she was, probably doing the most reckless thing she had ever done in her life, and the pedantic, efficient side of her was checking dates!

Making her way back to the bedroom, she gazed at Clem's outstretched body lying on the bed. Her heart was in her mouth but she couldn't help but gasp in admiration at the sight of him. Taut muscles subtly defined by the gentle bedside lamp. The silky shadow of ebony hair over his broad chest tapering into a fine line along his toned abdomen, edging downwards as if directing her to the very pinnacle of this beautiful man.

For once she had no reservations, no qualms, no self-doubt. Slowly, seductively she made her way to the bed. Kneeling astride him, she bent her head, her Titian curls tumbling onto his chest, her supple lips tenderly, teasingly exploring his torso. Boldly descending his rigid abdomen, relishing his scent, savouring the delicious salty tang of his skin on her lips, aware of her power as a woman.

She heard his sharp intake of breath as her lips moved lower still, teasing him until he could take it no more. In one supple movement Clem sat up, his strong arms engulfing her, laying her down on the rumpled sheets, the need to be inside her surpassing everything.

And then they were one, locked together in a rhythmic embrace that transcended all else, their bodies in blissful unison, driving each other on to a zenith that was as pure as it was magical.

Lying there, their bodies entwined, slowly the world

came back into focus—the ticking of a bedside clock, the ceiling fan delivering a welcoming gentle breeze on her warm, flushed skin. But just as suddenly as their intimacy had ignited it seemed to die. Olivia sensed his detachment even before he said a word.

'Clem?' Her voice was questioning, anxious, and his response did nothing to allay her fears. With a deep sigh he rolled onto his back and gazed at the ceiling, breaking the physical contact.

'Livvy, oh, Livvy.' His voice was deep, thick with emotion. He turned onto his side, propping himself on his elbow, and gently picked up her hand. 'I shouldn't have rushed you.'

Olivia shook her head. 'But you didn't. I thought it was what we both wanted?'

'It was, it is…' But it sounded to Olivia more as if he was trying to convince himself than her.

'Then what's wrong?' she demanded.

'Nothing's wrong, I just think we need to talk. Livvy, I never want you to regret a moment of our time together. I never want to hurt you, and without wanting to sound mercenary I won't let myself be hurt again.'

'What makes you think I'd hurt you?' she asked, bewildered.

He pulled her hand up to his face, his lips gently brushing her slender fingers. 'There was an engagement ring here not so long ago. We've both got so much emotional baggage I just think we should have cleared a few things up first, before we went this far.'

Suddenly she felt stupid. Acutely aware of her exposed breasts, she sat up and grabbed at the bedspread, pulling it around her. Never had she felt more vulnerable.

'There's no need to explain,' she said haughtily. 'I mean, I'm sorry if I forced you.' She knew she was being cruel, but she wasn't feeling very gracious. He had initiated things, he had asked her over and made love to her, and now he was calling a halt, telling her to slow down. Didn't she have any say here?

'Livvy, please, don't get upset. Just let me explain. You know I want you. It's just…'

'Just what?' Her voice was rising now. Olivia swallowed hard a couple of times. She wouldn't lose it here. The day had been bad enough without this. How dare he land this lot on her? 'Just that you thought you were ready, but now you're not sure? Or just, you thought I was? Well, I've got news for you, Clem. Make your mind up a bit earlier next time. I'm not a tap you can just turn on and off, I'm a woman!' In one movement she stood up, grabbing at her carelessly discarded clothes. In an instant he was beside her.

'Livvy, stop it.' His voice was firm without being harsh as he pulled her into his arms, holding her body stiff and unyielding against him. 'God, what did that bastard do to you? All I said was that we needed to talk,' he murmured into her hair, gently stroking her, gradually rekindling the intimacy and tenderness the night had held until finally she relented, relaxing against him, allowing herself to be comforted.

'All I was trying to say,' he repeated gently, 'was that we need to talk.'

'I know, I know.' She buried her face in the warm shelter of his chest. Olivia knew she had overreacted, and she knew he was right—they did need to talk, but not now. Jeremy, Kathy, Charlotte—they all had to be addressed, but surely it could wait?

She nodded, nestling into him. 'I know we do but, please, Clem, not tonight.'

Tenderly he drew her back onto the rumpled bed and back into his arms.

'I'm sorry I upset you,' he said softly. 'My timing can be lousy sometimes.'

'Oh, I don't know about that,' said Olivia huskily, running her long fingers lazily between his muscular thighs, boldly taking him in her hands and guiding him gently towards her. 'Your timing seemed perfect to me.'

Wrapped in his arms she slept so soundly even his pager didn't disturb her. Clem awoke her with a tender kiss.

'What time is it?'

'After one. I just got paged. Elsie Parker's taken a turn for the worse. There's not much I can do but I think it would help the family if I was there.'

Olivia nodded. Elsie Parker was in her late sixties and at the end of a long battle against ovarian cancer. 'Poor things. Is there anything I can do?'

Clem shook his head. 'I don't know how long I'll be. You go back to sleep, you look exhausted.'

'I'm all right, but I think I'd better go home. I don't really fancy waking up to find Ruby trying to make your bed.'

Clem laughed. 'Good point. The minute Ruby finds out, the whole town will know. It would be nice to get used to the idea ourselves first.' He squeezed her thigh through the sheet. 'You don't mind?'

Olivia shook her head 'No, you go.'

'I'll see you home.'

'Clem, I live two minutes away I can get there myself. Go and see how Elsie is doing—she needs you now.'

He smiled appreciatively and gave her a hurried kiss before he left. She lay there for a few moments after he had gone, remembering their love-making, her body tingling just at the memory of his touch, until finally, reluctantly she left the crumpled bed where they had finally found each other.

CHAPTER NINE

A SUDDEN violent spasm in Olivia's stomach awoke her. Retching, she just made it to the bathroom in time, a cold sweat drenching her. Leaning over the sink she rinsed her mouth from the tap and caught sight of herself in the mirror. Her face was pinched and pale, perspiration beading on her forehead, her eyes dark and sunken. She peered at her reflection. Imagine if she had stayed the night at Clem's—it was hardly a face to wake up to.

Gradually the pain eased to a dull ache and she made her way gingerly back to her bed. She looked over at her alarm clock—it was just after five. Surely the pizza would have been all right? It was only a frozen one, and it wasn't even as if she'd had a lot to drink—she hadn't even finished her glass of champagne.

Olivia drifted into an uneasy sleep, only to be awoken what seemed like seconds later by the sound of her alarm. She was no hero and under absolutely any other circumstances there was no way she would have even considered going into work. But given the developments of the previous night, what else could she do?

The thought of ringing Clem and saying she was too sick to come in was incomprehensible. He would misinterpret it as embarrassment or guilt. Their relationship was just too fragile and vulnerable to jeopardise at this tender stage. No. The music had to be faced. It was Friday. If she could just get through the morning then she'd have the whole weekend to recover and, anyway, she'd had far too much sick time already.

The pain in her shoulder made putting on make-up even

more difficult. Slapping on a great deal of foundation and blusher, she managed to look almost normal and made it to the surgery just ten minutes late. Thankfully, there were no patients waiting for her.

Betty greeted her warmly, obviously buoyed by the experience they had shared. 'Have you heard how the baby is? I wanted to ask Clem, but Mr Heath was already waiting and got in first.'

'Clem rang the hospital last night and they said he was stable. I would imagine he'll ring again this morning when he's got a minute. I'm just going to go into the treatment room to catch up on yesterday's files. Would you call if any patients come for me?'

Betty nodded. 'Would you like me to bring you in a coffee?'

She was obviously in the mood for a chat which was the last thing Olivia felt like, but she suddenly felt guilty, remembering how badly she'd needed to go over and over the birth. Betty must be feeling the same.

'Thanks, Betty, that would be lovely. Oh, and, Betty, I meant to thank you yesterday but I never got the chance. Your help was invaluable to me and I'm sure Lorna and Pete would say the same. I know Clem was pleased with you.'

'I did nothing,' replied Betty, blushing to the roots of her hair.

'Of course you did. Your actions bought us some time, which was what we were fighting for. What's this?' she added, pointing to a large jar on Betty's desk.

'I've organised a collection for Lorna and Pete—they'll be struggling, having to stay in Sydney. It's got off to a great start—everyone in the hotel chipped in.' The jar was crammed with notes and coins already, and the baby wasn't even twenty-four hours old.

Olivia felt a huge lump in her throat. Everyone was find-

g it tough here, the drought was really biting, and yet
ney still managed to chip in, sure in the knowledge that
thers were worse off. Only last week they had arranged a
uge convoy of trucks to take feed for the cattle up in
Queensland, knowing that if they thought they were strug-
ling here, the situation was dire further north. It was just
ne huge family and Olivia felt privileged to belong. She
ug into her purse and added a fifty-dollar note to the col-
ection.

'That's very generous,' Betty said. Olivia gave her a
mall wink.

'Jeremy can afford it,' she joked, thinking of the car she
ad sold to get her here.

Betty giggled and even Olivia laughed. Maybe she would
nake more of an effort with the receptionist.

'We're going to have a working bee next weekend to fix
p the house for them. Poor Pete had only got round to
uying the paint—they just moved in last week. I know
ou've been sick and we don't expect you to help with the
ouse, but maybe youse can knit something?'

Olivia nodded weakly. She had never held a knitting nee-
le in her life. 'Of course.' She made a mental note to write
o Jessica, and ask her to send a little matinée outfit. She
ould always tear out the label. A wave of nausea swept
ver her. 'I'll get started on those notes,' she said weakly,
scaping to the treatment room. Betty was far too pleased
vith the praise to notice Olivia's rapid departure.

As she sat at the desk the words blurred in front of her.
This was ridiculous—there was no way she should be at
vork. Maybe she had overdone things, what with the glan-
lular fever and then all the drama of yesterday. Clem would
nderstand. After all, hadn't he insisted she take it easy and
ell him if there were any problems? She would simply tell
im that she wasn't feeling well, and be totally professional
ut friendly. Her plans were to no avail, though. Walking

out into the waiting room, she promptly collided wit
Charlotte, who practically shoved Olivia out of the way i
her haste to get to Clem's room.

'I need to see Clem immediately!' she barked at Betty.

'He's in with a patient,' Betty retorted sharply. 'I'll le
him know you're here as soon as he's finished.'

'I don't care if he's in with the Queen of England,
Charlotte snarled. 'I need to see him this instant.' It too
all of Olivia's tact and even more of Betty's strength t
block the door and prevent her from barging in on M
Heath's prostate examination. Clem opened the door, en
raged.

'What the hell's going on?' he demanded.

'I need to see you, Clem. Now,' Charlotte begged loudly
but in a far more endearing tone.

Clem, realising he was obviously not going to be able t
calm Charlotte down without attending to her, looked ove
at Olivia. For an instant she felt a blush rise as she remem
bered the last time their eyes had met. 'Would you min
checking Mr Heath's blood pressure? If that's all right te
him I'll ring him at home this afternoon. Give him m
apologies.' Clem's voice was totally calm, as if this typ
of intrusion happened every day. He also looked disgust
ingly healthy, which ruled out the pizza being off.

Olivia nodded, suddenly irritated by this silly woman
who assumed she was so much more important than every
body else was. Clem turned to the drama queen.

'Charlotte, go and wait in my study. I'll be there in jus
a moment.' Charlotte, pacified now she had got her way
strutted off. 'Betty, would you hold my calls, unless, o
course, they're urgent?'

'But what'll I tell the patients that are waiting?' sh
asked. For the first time Clem sounded irritated. Charlott
must have got to him after all.

'Tell them something came up. It's not as if they don'

know. After all, Charlotte's outburst was hardly discreet. Tell them what you like.' And he marched off.

'Perhaps they were made for each other after all,' Betty muttered furiously.

Olivia tried to appease Mr Heath as she checked his blood pressure.

''Struth, I wanted to ask Clem for a script for me heart pills.'

'I'll have him write it up and I'll drop it in to the chemist for you this afternoon. He really is sorry. Something came up and he had to rush off.'

'I may be old, Sister, but I ain't deaf. That blooming sheila Charlotte calls and he runs. I dunno, she doesn't care tuppence for anyone except herself. What he's doing messin' with her I'll never know. Kathy must be turning in her grave, knowing that madam finally got her claws in him.' He waved a gnarled, arthritic finger at her. 'Nothing good will ever come of it, I tell you. She should stay put in Sydney, the city suits her.'

Olivia smiled noncommittally and helped the old man down off the examination couch. Privately she agreed with every word. Charlotte. She was like an unopened red bill, stuffed hastily into your handbag. Something, no matter how hard you tried, you never really forgot, but at least until you saw it you didn't have to deal with it. Well, the time had surely come. The music had to be faced, but not here, not at work. The next opportunity she got she would confront Clem, ask him outright just what was going on between him and Charlotte. The truth must surely be better than this uncertainty.

Finally Charlotte appeared, tearful but a lot calmer. Oliva tried to hover, to hear any snippet of their conversation, but a patient arrived, waving a pathology slip under her nose, and as there was no one else waiting for her, she really had

no choice but to get on with it. Clem walked Charlotte to
her car, hardly part of the service.

Olivia tried to concentrate as she took Mrs Peacock's
blood. Thankfully she had good veins and the needle went
in without difficulty.

'Well, that was nice and quick. It makes a change to be
seen straight away. Thanks for that.' She rolled down her
sleeve. 'Are you all right, Sister? You look a bit peaky.'

'I'm just a bit under the weather, nothing to worry
about.' Olivia gave her a smile. 'Those results should be
back early next week. If there are any problems, Clem or
I will call you.'

'No worries. Thanks, Sister. And you take care of yourself.'

Walking over to the window where the sharps bin was
kept, Olivia carefully emptied the kidney dish into the re-
ceptacle. Cursing herself for not being able to resist, she
stood on tiptoe and peeped out of the window into the car
park. And instantly wished she hadn't, for she was just in
time to see Clem gently embrace Charlotte. She was leaning against him, nodding. Olivia felt as if she had been
stabbed. She watched as he opened the car door and
Charlotte climbed into her sporty soft top—red, of course.
She was predictable. Olivia just ducked in time as Charlotte
sped off and Clem turned and walked back to the surgery.
She certainly didn't want Clem to catch her spying on him.

'What on earth was I thinking, getting involved with another man, let alone another doctor?' she muttered.

Clem walked into the treatment room. He had no reason
to be there unless he wanted to see her. He looked tired
but smiled when he spoke.

'I'm really behind now. How are you this morning?'
Gently he put his hand up to her cheek, but she pulled it
down and turned away, unable to take this display of affection. There were questions to be answered first. 'M

Heath needs a script for digoxin. I said I'd drop it into the chemist for him this afternoon,' Olivia said tonelessly.

'Thanks for that. I'd better write it up now or I'll forget, and I've already messed him about enough this morning.' He looked at her quizzically and suddenly his voice was serious. 'Livvy, are you feeling all right? You look ever so pale.'

I feel pale, she wanted to scream. I don't know if it's my stomach aching or my heart and head for being so stupid. Instead, she replied in the same toneless voice, 'I'm fine, just a bit tired. How's Elsie Parker?'

'Still battling on. She's amazing really. I've increased her morphine and changed her anti-emetic, which hopefully will make her more comfortable. I'll go and check on her this afternoon.'

Betty appeared at the door. 'The natives are getting restless.'

'I'm coming now.'

Betty bustled away.

'Livvy?'

'What?' she snapped. Clem just stood there. She didn't look at him, she couldn't bring herself to. Whatever he had been about to say, he obviously thought better of it.

'Never mind, it will keep till after surgery. I've left my prescription pad in the study. Would you mind bringing it in to me? I'll carry on with the patients.'

'Certainly.'

It was a beautiful study. Heavy wooden shelves lined the walls, every inch crammed with books, ranging from medical encyclopaedias and journals to various classics and the latest blockbusters. His huge, untidy desk sent Ruby into hysterics, but Clem knew where everything was and could place his hand on what he needed in an instant. Olivia, however, was not privy to his chaos. She rummaged through the various files and pieces of paper, eventually finding the prescription pad.

Picking it up, her heart skipped a beat, for lying there under it was a pregnancy test card. The blotting paper still paling showed it was a fresh test. What's more, it was positive! Her hands shot up to her mouth, stifling the scream that welled inside as the test card clattered to the floor.

How could he? How could he have done this to her? How could he have let her into his bed, into his life? It all made ghastly sense now—that was what this morning had been about. As friendly as Clem might be to his patients, that had been no doctor's congratulatory hug she had witnessed them sharing, and Charlotte's behaviour certainly wasn't one of a normal patient. Had she needed any more proof, Betty bustled in, bearing the final nail in the coffin.

'There you are. He's screaming for his pad. As if we don't have enough to deal with, he's now decided to head off to Sydney tomorrow morning, so I'll be on the phone all day, cancelling his weekend house calls. I hope he's back by Monday or we'll be stuck with old Dr Humphreys for surgery. It's bad enough when he's on call. Don't go getting sick this weekend—he'll kill us all, he's that old.'

Listening to Betty's ranting, Olivia swallowed the bile that rose in her throat. 'Why's Clem going to Sydney?' she asked, trying desperately to keep her voice even.

'And youse are supposed to have the brains. That's where madam lives, remember? I hope he's not going to propose. I mean it, I'll give him one week's notice.'

Numb now, she made her way back through the patient area. Clem's office door was open, and without bothering to knock she walked straight in and gave him the pad without a word.

'Thanks,' he muttered. Looking up, he saw her face and quickly came around the desk. 'Sit down. You really are pale.'

'I said I'm fine,' she snapped, near to tears and determined not to let him see.

'You don't look it.'

'Well, I am. How's Charlotte?' He was smooth—not even a flicker of guilt marred his concerned expression.

'Much calmer. She's off to Sydney, thank goodness. I'm just about sick of her dramas.' He sat down on the desk and gently picked up one of her slim hands. Olivia sat there frozen, her lips white, anger welling up inside her, only to be drowned by a huge wave of sadness for what might have been.

'Livvy, we really need to talk.'

'So you keep telling me, but we never seem to get there.' She damn well wasn't going to make this easy for him.

'I know. Look, I haven't been completely up front with you. I wanted to be sure about something before I bothered you with it, but things have suddenly started to happen—shall we say, a rather unexpected turn of events?'

Olivia's jaw dropped. Was that how he saw Charlotte's pregnancy? Some minor inconvenience to an otherwise normal day? But Clem continued talking, seemingly oblivious to her reaction. I have to go to Sydney tomorrow morning, but I really need to speak to you before I leave.'

'You've got patients waiting,' she pointed out.

'I know. What about tonight? I'll take you out for dinner. We can talk. I won't get sidetracked, I really need you to say yes.'

He was almost begging her. It was Jeremy all over. What did he think he could possibly say to her? That he wanted them both? Or that the baby was a mistake? Hadn't he listened to a word she'd said about Jeremy? Did he really think she'd be so stupid all over again?

'What about Charlotte?' There, she'd said it. She held her breath, scrutinising his face for a reaction.

'What about her? I told you, she's gone, she won't disturb us.'

Suddenly she couldn't bear the sound of his voice. It was
so kind, so convincing. Maybe she should go out with him,
hear what he had to say. Aware she was weakening, Olivia
stood up sharply. What did this man do to her? She needed
to get out, to think things through. She was scared, so
scared that she'd lose her head and accept his story, only
to be tortured all over again. 'Actually, you were right. I
don't feel well. I think I'm going to have to go home to
bed.'

'What's wrong?'

'I've probably just been overdoing things. Look, I'll take
a raincheck on dinner and grab an early night.'

'Let me have a look at you.'

He looked so worried, as if he really cared. Surely there
must be some explanation. Maybe he and Charlotte had had
a one-night stand for old time's sake. Maybe... No, she
reminded herself firmly, don't make excuses.

'No.' She almost shouted at him. 'I just need a rest. If
you'll excuse me.' And not even bothering to say goodbye,
she rushed out of the surgery, only stopping to grab her
bag.

When she got home Ruby was there, busily sweeping the
floorboards and desperate for news on the baby.

'You're early. Come on, I'll put the kettle on and we'll
have a nice cuppa. Youse can tell me all about the baby.
The way Betty's carrying on, it sounds like she delivered
it. She didn't, did she?'

Olivia shook her head. Normally she loved Ruby and
didn't mind whiling away the hours with her, but right now
she really needed to be alone.

'Ruby, I don't feel too good. I'm just going to go and
lie on the settee. Do you mind finishing up?'

Ruby fussed over her, laying her down and fetching a

pillow, but Olivia could tell she was hurt by her dismissal. 'Come over tomorrow morning,' Olivia suggested. 'I'll fill you in then. I really am tired.'

Appeased, Ruby tucked a rug around her. 'I knew it was too soon for youse to be back at work. You rest there, pet, and I'll get out of your hair. Can I get you a drink?'

'No, but thanks.'

Ruby hesitated. She really didn't want to leave. She'd never seen Olivia looking so awful, except those first couple of days after she'd gone missing.

'Is there anything I can do?'

'You could light a fire. I'm frozen.'

'But it's thirty degrees outside,' Ruby exclaimed, then, seeing Olivia shivering on the couch, she did as she'd been asked. Expertly arranging the wood, she lit a match and fanned the tiny flame till the fire burned merrily. 'Shall I fetch Clem? You look worse than you did fifteen minutes ago.'

'Ruby, please, don't.'

Ruby looked unsure, but Olivia insisted.

'I mean it. He knows I'm sick. That's why I came home early. I just need to rest. Promise me you won't go dragging him over.'

'Well, if you're sure…' She hovered for a moment then reluctantly packed up her things. 'Call if you need me.' She departed.

Olivia lay there for how long she wasn't quite sure, but gradually the room grew darker. Only the light from the ebbing fire filled the room, casting long shadows. Gazing into the glowing embers, she searched for answers.

How could she have let it happen? The last thing she had been looking for had been another relationship. Hadn't she only come to Kirrijong to straighten her head and stop her making a foolish mistake? Now Jeremy felt more like a distant memory than the man for whom she had wept such bitter tears. Instead she had gone and fallen completely in love with Clem.

'I love him,' she whispered to the dying flames. And somehow acknowledging the truth out loud made her feel calmer. Perhaps in a couple of months she'd be over Clem, too, but Olivia knew better. This was the thunderbolt, the once in a lifetime the world spoke about. He had made love to her, tapped wells of passions never explored. Opened the gateway to a nirvana she hadn't realised existed.

Yet how could she love him when she obviously didn't know him? The man she loved would never have been kissing her, making love to her, if he had Charlotte, however unwelcome, waiting in the wings. The Clem she knew would never have asked her out to dinner tonight if he'd just found out he was to become a father, even if it was, as she guiltily hoped, a mistake borne out of a brief fling. The Clem she loved would face the music and to heck with the consequences. He certainly wouldn't have let Charlotte speed off alone to Sydney.

Olivia's mind whirred. She simply didn't understand. Perhaps she had totally misjudged him and fallen in love with a fantasy figure; maybe it was a classic case of a patient falling for her doctor, or even just a rebound, to get her over Jeremy. If that was the case it had worked, but somehow it had backfired, for the cure was more agonising than the original disease. None of these excuses gave her any comfort yet the cold, hard truth was worse. She loved him, full stop, end of sentence. No ifs or buts, just a whole load of questions.

Yet did it really matter how she or even Charlotte for that matter felt? Whatever mess he had got himself into, Olivia was sure it was a reaction to his grief. Clem wasn't free to love either of them. His heart belonged to Kathy. How could she, with all her hang-ups and insecurities, even begin to compare with a woman who had been so perfect, trusting and gentle, the antithesis of herself? The only thing Kathy had done wrong had been to die and leave him, and it wasn't as if the poor woman had had a choice about that. Clem had his beloved memories. The ultimate other woman. How do you compete with a ghost?

The dull pain in her stomach spasmed suddenly, making her catch her breath. Olivia lay there in agony for a moment until gradually it eased. She was frozen to the core—perhaps a warm bath would help, she decided.

Watching the bath fill, she leant over to get the bubble bath but the pain in her shoulder intensified. The same nauseous feeling of the morning engulfed her. A spasm in her stomach hit her again, so violent it forced her to her knees, doubling her up on the bathroom floor. Something was wrong, terribly wrong.

Olivia tried to stand but her legs were trembling convulsively. She let out a whimper of pain and terror as she collapsed to the floor. 'Oh, God, help me, please.' She couldn't move, but just lay there, listening to the sound of running water, watching helplessly as the water lapped slowly over the edge of the bath. She had to get help. Had to get to the phone.

Slowly, so slowly, inch by inch, she dragged herself along the floor. The pain was so overwhelming, her muscles so fatigued, she was tempted just to lie there and rest a while, to let the bliss of oblivion descend on her, but an inner instinct, coupled with her training, told her she had to get to the phone. Had to let someone know of her plight. If she gave in, stopped now, then that would be it. The phone cord was just within her grasp and with a final, superhuman effort she stretched her fingers and pulled at the wire, bringing the phone crashing to the floor beside her.

The numbers were swimming before her eyes. Concentrating, trying desperately to focus, she somehow dialled Clem's number, praying she wouldn't get the answering machine or his voice mail.

'Clem speaking.' His voice sounded so calm, so normal. It was hard to believe he was unaware of the agony that was going on at the other end of the line. She tried to call his name but the words wouldn't come, just a tiny gasp. 'This is Clem. Is anybody there?'

She heard the urgency in his voice. Anyone else would have hung up, assuming a wrong number or a hoax call, but as a doctor this terrifying scenario had happened before.

'Clem,' she managed to croak, then inwardly cursed herself. If she had only one word left in her, why waste it telling him his name? But the heavens were listening and thankfully he recognised her voice.

'Livvy, Livvy, is that you?'

The fact he recognised her voice and the knowledge that help was on the way gave her some strength. 'Help me. Please,' she gasped.

'I'm on my way. Just stay there and don't move.'

She couldn't reply. The phone fell out of her limp hand and she lay there motionless on the floor, her breathing rapid and shallow, her skin deathly pale.

Clem frantically grabbed his medical bag and sprinted the short distance to the house, hammering loudly on the door, berating himself for not bringing the spare keys. Racing around to the side of the house, he saw Olivia through the bedroom window. Lying there so pale and still, he thought she must be dead.

In one movement he kicked out the window and opened the latch, desperate to reach her. Beside her in an instant, he saw she was still breathing. The relief was so intense he closed his eyes for a second and struggled to stay calm, then his sheer professionalism took over.

Her pulse was rapid and thready, she was so pale she

was practically exsanguinated. She was obviously, to his trained eye, bleeding out from somewhere.

He rang Betty, misdialling twice.

'G'day. Betty—'

'It's Clem, I'm at Livvy's,' he barked. 'She's critical. Organise an ambulance. Tell them we're going to need an airlift as well and that I'll ring with the details as soon as I can. Get Dougie and Ruby to come over now and tell them to bring the emergency blood from the fridge. Betty, hurry or we'll lose her.' He hung up, not waiting for a response, knowing Betty would come good when it mattered.

His training and experience were so ingrained that he treated Olivia methodically, managing to insert a drip into her hopelessly collapsed veins and squeeze lifesaving plasma substitute into her.

Dougie and Ruby arrived, horrified by what they saw. Clem was leaning over Olivia's inert body, oblivious of the pool of water they were both in from the overflowing bath. Dougie ran and turned off the taps as Ruby rushed over with the blood.

'Tell me what to do.'

'Squeeze this drip through. I'll get another IV line started and get the blood into her. Don't move her—she may have fallen. I don't think so but I'll put on a cervical collar to stabilise her neck just in case.'

Betty, with wisdom and insight that defied her scatty nature, arrived then, dragging the portable oxygen cylinder. She was purple from the exertion.

Clem looked at her gratefully. 'Good work Betty.' He slipped a green oxygen mask over Olivia's face, and for a fleeting second her eyes flickered.

Frantically Clem grabbed her hand. 'Livvy, Livvy, it's all going to be fine. We're getting you to hospital now.' In desperation he turned to Ruby. 'Did you see her eyes move? Do you think she can hear?'

And in that second Ruby knew. This wasn't a doctor speaking, this was a frantic man. His face held the same intense pain she had seen two years before. How clearly she remembered the week before Kathy had died, when she had taken her final turn for the worse. Betty had come running then, too, with the oxygen.

She knew then that Clem loved Olivia. They all did. In the months she had been there they had all grown to love and care for this tall, awkward, icy woman who could be so uptight and distant one minute and as vulnerable as a child the next. To see her lying there now, so fragile and helpless... Oh, poor, poor Clem. It must be like waking from a nightmare, only to be plunged straight back into the same hell all over again. He couldn't lose Livvy, too. God couldn't be that cruel.

They all battled with their emotions as they watched her limp body. Dougie coughing noisily to cover up his tears, leaving when the road ambulance arrived to help Bruce prepare a landing pad and light the flares. Ruby stood, trying to stay calm, with her hand on Clem's shoulder as he knelt over Olivia, oblivious of the ambulance officers working around him.

Betty had no such reserve and sobbed openly. 'What happened, Clem? What happened?'

He shook his head slowly. 'I'm pretty sure she's got a ruptured spleen.' His voice was quiet, flat.

'But how?' Betty's hysteria magnified Clem's frozen calm. 'Did she fall?'

'I don't think so. Glandular fever can cause an enlarged spleen. Very rarely it ruptures. I think that's what has happened to Livvy.'

'She will make it, though, won't she? I mean there's things they can do for that?'

Clem shrugged, utterly defeated. 'She needs more blood. She needs surgery, preferably half an hour ago. We've done all we can. It's out of our hands now.'

It took just over an hour for the helicopter to arrive from the base hospital, but it seemed like an eternity. They nearly lost Olivia twice, but just as it all looked hopeless the whirring of the chopper blades seemed to inject some hope into them all. Even Olivia stirred slightly and opened her eyes. She tried to focus on Clem's face, and for all his intuition he mistook the love that somehow shone in her dull, sunken eyes as gratitude for finding her again.

'You're going to be fine. The helicopter's here now.'

She tried to shake her head. That wasn't what she wanted to hear. She wanted him to tell her he loved her, to tell him she loved him, even if it was all too late. She tried to speak, but her mouth wouldn't obey her and only a small gasp came out.

'Hush, Livvy, don't try to talk now. We're all here. Everything will be all right. You have to trust me.'

And despite all the questions left unanswered, all the uncertainty, she did, no matter what.

His beautiful strong face was the last thing she saw as once again oblivion descended.

CHAPTER TEN

THANKFULLY Olivia knew nothing of the helicopter ride to Sydney. In a no-win situation they bypassed the nearer base hospital, after being informed the theatres were in use and the intensive care unit was full. They all knew that if Olivia was to stand any chance of survival she would need the best intensive care available. Bag after bag of blood was squeezed into her *en route,* as Clem knelt on the floor holding her lifeless hands, terrified that if he let go then so might she.

As the city lights neared and the crew expertly prepared her for a speedy exit from the helicopter, he had no choice but to let go. Helpless, he watched as the doors opened and she was rushed away. He wanted to run after her, to shout to them to do their best, that they couldn't lose her, she was far too precious. But his voice was lost in the whirring chopper blades, and all he could do was make his way to the theatre waiting room. He had told them all he could about her condition, all they needed to know.

The fact he loved her didn't matter to them. Everybody was someone's child or parent, lover or friend. All life was valuable, and they would give Olivia their best shot, in the same way he did each day, the same way Olivia did.

While he was sitting in the lonely waiting room, drinking endless cups of revolting machine coffee, a receptionist came in and asked for details. Gently she tried to get information out of him, but all Clem could manage was Olivia's name and current address. He didn't even know her date of birth. He loved this woman with every inch of is being and yet he couldn't even answer the most simple of questions about her.

'I'm sorry,' the receptionist answered, confused when he stalled on her date of birth. 'I thought you were the next of kin.'

'I'm her doctor.'

'I see,' she answered, still none the wiser. Doctors didn't normally pace the floors and cry openly over their patients, not to the receptionist anyway. 'Is there any way you'd be able get the information?'

He gave her Betty's number—she could pull out Livvy's résumé. 'I want to be informed the minute she gets out of Theatre,' he said, trying to regain his composure.

'Of course, Doctor.' The receptionist turned to walk out.

'She isn't just a patient to me, you know,' Clem called to her departing back, though why he had to justify himself to her he wasn't sure. 'I love her.'

The receptionist turned. She was used to grief. 'So I gathered. I hope things go well.' She smiled sympathetically. 'She's got the best surgical team on tonight. If it was any loved one that was sick, they're whom I'd want to be operating. Well, from what I hear anyway.' She blushed, suddenly remembering she was talking to a doctor.

'Thank you,' Clem said simply, glad that even though it had been to a relative stranger, he had at least acknowledged his love for Olivia.

The wait was interminable. Never had he felt so helpless. He knew, and yet couldn't bear to think of, the battle that would be going on in the sterile theatre. The wheels of bureaucracy would have swung into motion and by now Jeremy would have been contacted.

Jeremy. He had never met him, only spoken to him on the telephone, and yet he hated him with a passion. Hated him for causing Livvy so much pain. The bastard hadn't even had the decency to marry her yet he was listed on her résumé as the emergency contact. He was probably on his way now. Clem just hoped he had stopped to inform her parents in England.

His heart went out to them and the terrible events that would unfold when they picked up the phone and heard the devastating news. Would they all come? Was he going to meet the people who had made up Livvy's world before she'd come to Kirrijong? Beautiful, complicated Livvy.

Sitting in the bland waiting room, the television playing an old black and white film, he stared blankly at the screen. The film ended and a newsbreak followed. How could it not be the headlines? Why were they talking about some attempted bank robbery when his beloved Livvy was fighting just to stay alive?

Standing as he saw someone dressed in theatre blues approach, Clem tried to interpret the grim, weary face before she spoke, desperate for a clue.

'Dr Clemson.' She held out her hand and Clem shook it. 'I'm May Fordyce, the consultant surgeon on tonight. I operated on your patient.' The formalities over, Clem knew the news was coming and for a second he didn't want to hear it, terrified in case Livvy hadn't made it.

'She's more than a patient.' It was only fair to warn her. He didn't want the details to be too graphic.

Miss Fordyce nodded briefly. 'Your initial diagnosis was correct. She had indeed ruptured her spleen.'

'Is she…?'

'No,' she replied, but there was no jubilation in her voice. 'She made it through Theatre, but really I'm amazed she did. She's lost a lot of blood and she's had a massive transfusion. We're worried about disseminated intravascular coagulation.'

She waited for a response, for some recognition to flicker in Clem's eyes. Then she realised she wasn't speaking to another doctor but a scared and desperate fellow human being, and gently spelt the grim news out.

'You and the air ambulance team did a marvellous job of resuscitating her with fluids. When she arrived in Theatre we performed an urgent splenectomy. She made it through but she's critical. She's extremely weak and the volume of the blood transfusion is causing a lot of concern. We're having a lot of problems with her blood coagulation and we're trying to prevent her from going into renal failure. The next forty-eight hours will be crucial.'

A hundred questions flashed into Clem's mind, but for now the answers were immaterial. The need to see her, to touch her, surpassed everything. 'Can I see her?'

'They're just settling her into Intensive Care. I'll let them know you're waiting.'

For ten minutes he was allowed to see her. Just ten precious minutes. Gently he held her hand and told her all the things he had meant to say but somehow had never quite managed. Ten precious minutes where he told her just how much he cared and how happy she had made him, maybe without even realising it, and that he was sorry, so sorry that he couldn't have done more. Could she hear? There was no way of knowing but he knew that he had to say it now, for it might be his only chance.

Lovingly he arranged her long red curls. Walking over to the sink, he moistened a hand towel and wiped away a streak of blood that had splashed her cheek. 'You'd have me for breakfast if I left it,' he whispered gently into her ear.

'We need to do some obs.' The sister hovered by the bed. 'And she needs to rest.'

'I won't get in the way, I'll just sit here, if you don't mind.'

The Sister hesitated, not sure of this situation. Was he her doctor, friend or lover? Whatever he was, he seemed nice, and she felt it only fair to warn him. 'Her fiancé has flown in from Melbourne, he just arrived. Miss Fordyce is talking to him now. I expect he may want to sit with her.'

'Her ex-fiancé,' Clem stated bluntly but it was no use. In just one short sentence he had been relegated. For a moment Clem had the craziest notion to pick Olivia up and just run. He didn't want to leave, didn't want Jeremy or anyone else invading, but he didn't have any say here. And the hardest part to take was that he wasn't sure whether Livvy would have wanted him to.

Olivia was the talk of the intensive care staffroom. Two doctors in love with the same woman. One blond, with film-star good looks and a slick charm, who flirted with the staff and praised them for their efforts. The other dark and ruggedly handsome, but moody and picky, questioning every test result, checking the obs charts. Both as different as chalk and cheese, each with a bristling loathing of the other.

Over the weekend Olivia mercifully gradually stabilised and, defying all odds, by Monday was ready to be moved to a small side ward on the high-dependency unit, an array of wires and monitors still adorning her, each relaying its vital messages to the nurses' station. It was here that she started to drift back to the world. Her eyes heavy, she opened them slowly, flinching at the late afternoon sun that flooded the bed. Her throat felt dry and sore, as if it had been roughly sandpapered, her arm, strapped to the intravenous giving set, heavy and unfamiliar.

She felt a hand on her head and a familiar voice welcoming her back to the world.

'Darling, it's all right. You're coming to. Take it easy. You're in hospital but I'm here now and everything's going to be all right.'

'Be careful what you wish for—it might come true.' It seemed that Clem's prediction had finally come to fruition.

for there, coming into focus, his blond hair white in the
fluorescent light's glare, his face smiling down at her, was
Jeremy. Battling with nausea and pain, she tried to make
some sense, to orientate herself, the numerous drips and
machines all so familiar yet so alien now they were attached to her own body.

'Jeremy?' she croaked.

'Yes, it's me. I'm here now and I'm never going to let
you go again.'

'What happened?' she asked feebly.

'Your spleen ruptured. It would have been enlarged from
the glandular fever. It's very rare but it happened. I just
feel so guilty.'

He had a lot to feel guilty about. Olivia could recall that
much.

'I should have come and got you sooner, never left you
in the middle of nowhere with an out-of-date bush quack.
I'm sorry, darling.'

Olivia didn't respond. Instead, she lay there, trying to
piece it all together. With the benefit of hindsight, everything made sense now. That niggling pain in her shoulder,
the dizzy spells. Her medical mind realised they had been
signs she had been bleeding internally. The abdominal pain,
which she had just assumed to be food poisoning, had, in
fact, been her dangerously enlarged spleen leaking slowly,
with the potential to rupture at any time. But with hindsight
it was easy to diagnose. It had been no one's fault. She
could hardly point the finger at Clem when she had point-
blank refused to let him examine her, and she had avoided
a proper examination with Dr Humphreys. Anyway, surely
no one would have envisaged what was, after all, an extremely rare complication of a common viral disease.

So now here she lay, with Jeremy playing the part of the
concerned fiancé to perfection, saying all the things that a
few months ago she would have longed to hear. It was

almost farcical. A more dramatic reunion she couldn't have dreamed of. Totally inappropriately, and to Jeremy's absolute horror, Olivia started to laugh. He jumped back as if he'd been shot.

'She's confused. It must be all the pethidine you've loaded her up with,' he barked at the entering nurse, the Mister Nice Guy routine quickly starting to evaporate.

Olivia drifted in and out of consciousness. Once when she opened her eyes she saw Clem gazing down at her. He looked exhausted. The tiny lines around his eyes seemed deeper and they shone with tears. She wanted so badly to talk to tell him how she felt, but she had just had a shot of painkiller and its effects were starting to take hold, the words coming out muddled and confused.

'Shh. Not now,' was all he said, and gently placed a finger to her lips. 'You rest.'

When she awoke she was sure she must have dreamed the encounter, for there beside her was Jeremy. 'Hello darling. You've been out for hours.'

'What time is it?'

'Nearly seven. I was just waiting for you to wake up. I'm going to head off to the hotel and get some dinner. It's been a long day.' So he was complaining now. It wasn't as if she had asked him to come. 'But I've got some good news. I spoke with your surgeon and she's going to arrange your transfer to Melbourne in a couple of days. Get you back on home ground and amongst familiar faces. That's just what you need.'

'And you wouldn't have to take any time off work,' she added sarcastically.

'Olivia, don't let's fight. I thought that was all behind us now.' He kissed her haphazardly on the cheek. 'I'll let the sister know you're awake—they want to change your dressing. I'd just be in the way. Goodnight, darling. I'll be here first thing.'

Olivia nodded feebly. She had to tell him he was wasting his time, but right now she couldn't deal with a scene. It could wait till tomorrow morning.

Expertly, Sister Jay changed her dressing. She was middle-aged and incredibly efficient, with a brisk, rather old-school bedside manner. Olivia lay there, staring at the ceiling, thinking of what she would say to Jeremy, as the sister completed her task and deftly tidied up the bedclothes. After checking Olivia's pulse, she gently patted her hand and for a moment her face softened.

'You're looking a lot better. You were pretty crook there for a while, gave us all a fright.' Bustling out with the trolley, she returned a moment later. 'Are you up to a visitor?'

Olivia nodded. What did Jeremy want now? But standing in the doorway was Clem. He looked as tired and as awful as she felt.

'You look like it should be you in a hospital bed.' She smiled.

'They've put me up in the doctors' quarters. It's not bad, but I'd forgotten just how noisy they could be. There was a wild party on Saturday night—it went on till four a.m.'

'Did you go?'

He knew she was teasing but he played along. 'Just for a couple of hours, but the girls were awful and the beer was warm.' He came and sat gently on the bed, careful not to make any sudden movement that might cause her pain. Tentatively he took her hand and it felt so natural she left it there. 'I've actually spent the last few days and nights loitering around the corridor, waiting for Jeremy to leave. I'm surprised I haven't been arrested. I needed to see you were all right for myself. I came in once but you were out of it.'

So he had been here after all. It hadn't been a dream.

'I know what time it is, roughly to the nearest hour, but what day is it?'

Clem smiled at her question. 'It's Tuesday.'

'And you're still here. Why?' Suddenly she remembered that Charlotte was in Sydney. Of all the stupid things to ask. He had been coming here anyway.

'That's what I wanted to talk to you about.'

It was all too much—she simply wasn't up to hearing it. 'Not now, please.' Pulling her hand away, she turned her head towards the window and stared at the bland beige curtains.

'You're tired, of course. You need your rest. Can I come and see you again?'

What was the point? But somehow she needed to hear some answers, no matter how much it hurt. She had to find out all the details, but not tonight. 'Jeremy's coming in the morning,' she said.

'I see,' Clem answered, and she could hear the defeat in his voice.

'But he won't be staying long,' she added. 'Perhaps around lunchtime?'

Clem nodded. 'I'd like that.' Gently he stroked her cheek, but she couldn't take it, too scared she might crumble. Instead, she turned her face back to the curtains.

'I really thought I was going to lose you,' he murmured.

For a second she wavered, desperate to feel his arms around her, but common sense won.

'Thank you for saving me,' she said tonelessly, and then felt awful, for despite everything else this man had saved her life. She turned and looked at him. 'Thank you,' she said with more conviction.

Clem gave her a quizzical look. 'I'll let you rest. Till tomorrow, then.'

Olivia awoke next morning to the sound of the breakfast trolley. The 'Hourly sips' sign above her bed had been replaced by 'Free fluids'. Never had a weak cup of insipid hospital tea tasted so good. Gradually the tubes and drips had been taken down and all that was left to show of her near brush with death was one small drain, a dressing on her stomach and one peripheral intravenous line.

Being a nurse had some advantages. She was now officially well enough to be moved down into the shared ward away from the nurses' station, but while the ward was relatively quiet they left her in the side room. Replacing the cup in the saucer, she contemplated whether to ask for a second, but knew she shouldn't push it. Strange how the simplest things gave the most pleasure. The orderly came and pulled back the curtains.

'You've got the best view in the hospital here.' A huge gum nut tree filled almost the entire window. 'Enjoy it. When you get moved it's the furnace to look at.'

With mounting trepidation she dreaded Jeremy's arrival. She didn't have to wait long.

'Morning, darling, you look better.' Jeremy waltzed in, looking as immaculate as ever. 'I might even talk to Miss Fordyce and see if they can transfer you today. It's not as if they're doing much for you now and, anyway, I'll be in the ambulance with you. I am a consultant surgeon after all.'

Olivia listened, silently fuming. Jeremy just assumed he could pick up and carry on exactly where he had left off. Didn't she have any say in this?

'Actually, I won't be going back to Melbourne.' The words tumbled out and Olivia held her breath.

'Why?' he answered, nonplussed. 'Were you ill in the night? Is there something they haven't told me?'

'No, Jeremy. It's something you didn't ask me.'

He stared at her, completely confused.

'You just assume that I've forgiven you. You just assume

that I'm coming home with you. Well, I'm sorry, it's not that straightforward.'

He was over to the bed in a flash. 'We've been over that. It's all over with Lydia. You know how sorry I am.'

She almost felt sorry for him. He was so spoilt, so used to unquestioning adoration that it hadn't seriously entered his head that she might not come back to him.

'It's not about whether it's over with Lydia or not. It's the fact it happened in the first place. Jeremy, I'm sorry, I just can't forgive and forget—it's over.'

Jeremy shook his head. 'No, Olivia. Don't do this.'

A student nurse appeared and started to take her blood pressure. Intimidated to be in the room with such a senior nurse and doctor, she kept blowing the cuff up too tight.

'For heaven's sake don't they teach you anything in nursing school?' Jeremy snapped.

'She's doing fine.' Olivia smiled reassuringly.

Once they were alone again, he begged her to reconsider. 'Please, Olivia, I've changed, I promise. Once we're married you'll see—'

'No! *You* did this to us, Jeremy. I would have always been faithful, I would have supported you in anything, but I can't get over your affair. It's just too big. It's over, Jeremy.' She saw the tears well in his eyes and she knew he was devastated.

'You might change your mind,' he begged.

'I won't,' she replied firmly.

Jeremy shook his head. 'There's someone else. That Jake Clemson. I knew it. What's been going on?'

'This has nothing to do with him,' Olivia answered sincerely, because it didn't.

'I don't believe you,' Jeremy stated bluntly. 'Are you two having an affair?'

'No,' she answered truthfully, though such was her honesty that she told him the painful truth. 'But we did sleep together, once. It meant far more to me than it did to him—he's involved with someone else. And, anyway, this has nothing to do with Clem. It's about us.'

'Oh, I'd say he had a fair bit to do with it,' he retorted angrily, then the rage in him seemed to die as he begged her to reconsider. 'Please, Olivia,' he implored, but his pleas fell on deaf ears. It was simply too late.

Even her name sounded strange now. He was the only person who had called her 'Olivia' in ages. Even 'Livvy' was underlined on all her medical notes, a legacy of her admission when Clem had attempted to give her details. The Olivia Jeremy had known didn't exist any more. In her place was a stronger person, who would fight for her ideals.

'I'm sorry, Jeremy.' And something about the certainty in her voice made him finally realise she meant it. For a second the anger re-emerged and flashed over his face, but it soon subsided into a look of total defeat.

'I'm sorry, too, Olivia. Sorry for everything.' He stood there for a moment, taking in the enormity of the situation. Finally realising what he had lost. 'Do you want me to go?'

She nodded, biting her lip to stop the tears.

'Can I ring in a couple of days? See how you're getting on?'

Again she nodded and managed a faint smile. 'That would be nice.' She meant it. Hopefully they could go about this in a civilised way, remain friends even.

He left then, and Olivia turned her face and wept into the pillow, knowing how awful he felt, knowing that despite Jeremy's actions he had loved her, but just not enough.

Wiping away the tears, she let out a gasp. The old gum was full of bright reds and greens. A flock of rosellas was feasting on the tree. For a second she was transported back to Kirrijong, sitting by the tiny stream, pondering her future. So what now? Where did she go from here? She couldn't go back to Kirrijong. It would be torture, seeing Clem every day, knowing he was with Charlotte. Watching her blossom, ripe with pregnancy, heavy with Clem's child.

For a second she considered going back to Melbourne, but only for a second. Her time there was finished. It would take a stronger person than her to return there and work alongside her ex-fiancé. She could even return to England. Now that the panic was over her parents had rung, saying they would wait a couple of weeks till they flew out. Although longing to see them, she was actually grateful for the reprieve. She wasn't exactly bursting with places they could stay!

The uncertainty of her future was a problem that for now could wait. First she had to get this morning over with. Saying goodbye to Jeremy had been hard, but she had already expended most of her grief about their break-up. But saying goodbye to Clem, that was another matter altogether.

Sister Jay appeared in the doorway, carrying a familiar stainless-steel kidney dish.

'Time for your pethidine injection, and when that's taken effect I was wondering if you'd mind if Hannah, the student, gave you your blanket bath. She needs to be assessed, but she goes to pieces if anyone watches her. I thought she might feel less threatened if I left her to it, and perhaps you could let me know how she does?'

Olivia agreed, though she doubted whether the poor girl would be any less intimidated after Jeremy's outburst.

'That's fine, but I don't want the injection, thanks.'

Sister Jay checked Olivia's prescription chart.

'Are you sure? It's been a while since your last one and you're still written up for regular analgesia. The physiotherapist is coming later to sit you out of bed, which is going to hurt. Don't try to be brave. You've been through a lot.'

But Olivia was adamant. 'Really, I'd rather not.'

Sister Jay shrugged and left.

Her stomach hurt, it hurt like hell, but the pain was nothing compared to seeing Clem for what was to be the last time. She wanted a clear head for that. Wanted to be sure she understood everything he said. It was also imperative to her that she memorised his face. If she was going to live the rest of her life on dreams, she at least wanted them to be accurate.

Hannah clattered in, blushing furiously as she pushed a huge trolley laden with jugs and various pieces of linen and toiletries.

'I've come to give you a wash,' she ventured nervously.

Olivia's heart went out to the young woman. Nurses hated looking after other nurses at the best of times, and poor Hannah had drawn the short straw. Wincing with pain, Olivia leant over and opened the bedside drawer. Nothing, not even a comb.

Hannah set to work and Olivia lay there, pretending not to notice the tepid water splashing her face and trickling into her ears. Lying on her side as Hannah gingerly washed her back, she eyed the goodies on the trolley. Fern-scented talcum powder, pink carbolic soap—hardly the stuff to bring Clem to his knees. Not, she reminded herself firmly, that that was on the agenda.

'Just stay there. I forgot to get the lanolin cream for your pressure areas.' Hannah hastily covered her with a towel.

'Just a moment,' Olivia called. 'Hannah, I know it's awful for you, having to bathe me, and you're doing marvellously,' she added as the young girl's eyes widened, anticipating criticism. 'But what I really need, more than anything else, is to feel human again. Is there anything in the store cupboard that doesn't reek of disinfectant? And is there any chance of borrowing someone's mirror? I know I look a sight and obviously I didn't bring anything with me.'

Hannah started to smile. 'Are you expecting a visitor?' she asked perceptively.

It was Olivia's turn to blush. 'Well, sort of.'

'Then we'd better get you sorted. I shan't be long.'

Hannah returned moments later with her own make-up bag. 'When Sister Jay asks, I gave you the best blanket bath ever.'

'Absolutely. The best,' Olivia agreed as she rummaged through the bag. They even shared the same taste in perfume.

Hannah combed the knots out of her hair, while Olivia shakily managed a touch of mascara on her lashes and a dash of blusher. She knew she must still look awful but it was a huge improvement. Hannah had found what was probably the only hospital gown that actually had all the ties and didn't constantly fall off your shoulders. A quick spray of perfume and she felt close to human again.

'Thank you so much.'

'No worries.' Hannah smiled, confident now the barriers had been broken down. 'I'll just do your obs and then I'll leave you.'

For all her inexperience Hannah wasn't stupid. As she took Olivia's pulse, Clem arrived. Feeling her patient's heart rate suddenly accelerate, she knew it had nothing to with the operation. She quickly wrote down the obs and with an almost imperceptible wink she left them alone, gently closing the door behind her.

'How on earth do you manage it?' Clem laughed. 'You've been to hell and back and you still manage to come out looking gorgeous.'

'Hardly gorgeous,' Olivia replied lightly, 'but I certainly do feel much better today.'

'I've just been talking to some fans of yours.'

'Who?'

'Lorna and Pete. Our namesake is on the next floor.'

'Our namesake?'

'Baby Oliver Jake. He's doing very well.' Olivia leant back on the pillow.

'Oliver Jake,' she repeated. 'They didn't have to do that. He's doing well, you say?'

'Exceptionally. It's still very early days and there's a long way to go, of course, but all the signs look good. They want to pop down and visit you, but I said to give it a couple of days.'

Olivia nodded. Finally some good news.

'That would be nice. I expect I shan't be inundated with visitors. When are you going back?'

He sat down on the bed, achingly close. She so badly wanted to reach out and touch him, but kept her hands firmly beside her.

'That depends. I've managed to arrange a locum.'

'Dr Humphreys? Are you sure that's such a good idea?'

Clem shook his head.

'No, I've actually hired someone who's seriously considering the job of running the hospital. It's worked out well. It gives him a chance to see whether it's what he wants to do, and if it is, he can have his say in the final touches to the hospital.' He looked closely at her, watching her reaction as realisation struck.

'But I thought you'd be running it,' she said slowly, utterly confused.

'I know you did. That's what I've been trying to talk to you about.'

Her mind raced.

'I was actually coming to Sydney at the weekend to have dinner with an old friend and colleague, Craig Pryde— though I wasn't expecting to travel by helicopter,' he added.

Olivia stared dumbly at him.

'You know how I missed paeds?' he said gently.

Speechless, she nodded.

'Well, I've known Craig for many years. He's a paediatric consultant here at this hospital. He's going to be retiring next year, and his senior registrar just resigned unexpectedly. He's asked me to consider the position. When Craig retires I'd probably be offered the consultant's position. It's a great opportunity.'

Agonisingly slowly, realisation dawned. His future was moving on and she hadn't even been in the picture. Of course he would come here. Charlotte would never stay permanently in Kirrijong.

Olivia's pledge to concentrate and remember every word quickly went out of the window. Fighting just to hold back the tears as Clem went into detail, she was unable to take in the rest of what he was saying.

'So what do you think?' Clem concluded.

Olivia swallowed hard and forced her eyes to meet his, determined to retain at least a shred of dignity. 'It's a bit of a shock, I admit, but if you're sure it's what you want then go for it.'

She tried to sound pleased for him, to inject some enthusiasm, but it was asking too much. Maybe she should have had the pethidine after all.

'But this isn't just about me. I need to know how you feel.'

'Why?' she asked simply. Her feelings didn't come into it. Shouldn't he be having this conversation with Charlotte?

'Livvy, haven't you heard a word I've been saying?'

Olivia shook her head dumbly.

'I wanted to discuss it with you but it all happened so quickly and we never did seem to get around to having that talk. Then you were taken so ill. I've been trying to ask you to come with me. I know you've got Jeremy to consider and I didn't want to interfere, but I can't sit on the fence any longer. I know we haven't had much time to-

gether but surely you feel it, too?' His words tumbled out
and for once he wasn't the strong, confident Clem she
knew.

It was Olivia who spoke calmly. 'Jeremy and I are finished. We have been for ages. It just took a while for him
to get used to the idea,' she said.

Hope flickered in his eyes then faded as he saw the look
of confusion on her face. 'This surely can't be that much
of a shock. You must know some of how I feel? I've been
trying to tell you for long enough.'

'I know about Charlotte. The baby, I mean.' She held
her breath.

'How?' he asked, bewildered.

'I found the pregnancy test card.'

'But that's got nothing to do with us.'

Olivia put her hands up to her ears, trying to block out
the sound of his voice. She couldn't bear it. Couldn't bear
to hear the excuses and lies. 'Oh, I'd say it had rather a lot
to do with us, or maybe I'm just being old-fashioned. But
I still think a baby needs a father. I thought we'd at least
agree on that.' She stared defiantly at him, waiting for the
excuses, the pathetic attempt at an explanation. She was
stunned to see his look of incredulous shock change to one
of anger—not the usual flashes of temper she had grown
used to but a black rage that descended on his tired face.
And what was even more disturbing was that she saw the
disappointment in his eyes.

'You think it's my baby?' His lips were white, set in a
thin line. 'How could you think that of me?' he rasped.
'How could you, Livvy? Is that the kind of guy you take
me for?'

This wasn't a reaction she had anticipated. Agonisingly,
realisation dawned. She had made the biggest mistake of
her life.

'What else was I to think?' she answered defensively.

'Obviously you didn't think. You just assumed. Hell, I know you've been hurt, but how dare you tar me with the same brush as Jeremy?'

'I didn't want to,' she pleaded, 'but it seemed so obvious. Ruby said—'

'I don't care what Ruby said,' he replied sharply, trying desperately not to shout. 'I told you never to listen to her. Why didn't you ask me?'

'I did. I asked if there'd ever been anyone since Kathy.'

He looked at her perplexed. 'Go on.'

'And you said, "What do you think?"' she responded lamely, knowing how inadequate her excuse sounded.

'So it was easier to assume that I was sleeping around. "What do you think?" "What do you think?"' His voice was rising now. 'My heavens, couldn't you see what I was trying to tell you? Since Kathy died I haven't been able to focus, let alone look at another woman—until you, that is. That night when I came to your door drunk I was terrified. Terrified because I knew I'd fallen in love and you seemed so wrapped up in Jeremy. Terrified because I finally knew it was time to move on.'

'But you used to go out with Charlotte. Surely you can see why I thought—'

'Oh, please.' He stopped her flood of excuses. 'One town dance fifteen years ago does not constitute a relationship, unless, of course, you're listening to gossip,' he said nastily. Then, seeing her start to cry, he let up.

'Charlotte's baby has nothing to do with me,' he finally explained, 'save the fact it will be my niece or nephew. She's got herself mixed up with Joshua, my brother, and I've been acting as an unwilling go-between. She's here in Sydney now, hoping he'll relent and marry her. The poor kid, it will probably turn out an absolute horror with those two spoilt brats as parents.'

What could she say? To have been so terribly wrong.

'Sorry' just didn't seem enough. All this time he had been trying to tell her he loved her while she had been thinking the worst.

'So you never slept with Charlotte?' She hesitated, taking in the enormity of what Clem was telling her. 'I was the first since Kathy.' Their one magical night together was suddenly magnified. She felt privileged and also painfully guilty, for Clem had been right—they *had* rushed things. She should have known that it had been his first time since Kathy. She should have been aware that, despite the joy and tenderness they had shared when they'd made love, there would have also been some pain and recrimination for Clem. No wonder he had seemed detached after they'd made love. No wonder he had needed to talk. It was something she should have known.

Seeing Olivia lying there utterly desolated, Clem felt his anger evaporate. This was hurting her as much as him, and the last thing he wanted was to cause her more pain.

'Yes, Livvy, you were the first since Kathy, and I hope the last. I can never go through this again. I've loved you from the moment I met you. I wasn't looking—in fact, I nearly ran a mile—but I couldn't escape it. It's just taken a while for me to get used to the idea. I was so sure I was going to spend the rest of my life alone, and then you came along. For the first time in ages there was a reason to get up in the morning, a face I wanted to see, and someone's opinion I wanted to hear. And it terrified me.'

Olivia lay there, slowly taking in what he was telling her.

'I know it's asking a lot for you to move your life here so I can chase a dream job. And before you even think it, it's not a "consultant's wife" I'm after. It's you, Livvy, and it always will. I know you're going to need some time to think about it but, please, hear me out first. I can be so bloody-minded sometimes and I know I can be unreasonable, but I truly love you. I'd never hurt you.' He ran a shaking hand through his hair.

She felt like the judge and jury listening to the closing argument.

'I want to marry you, take care of you and show you that love can be good. But, Livvy, if you can't trust me, if you're unable to believe in all we could be together, we should forget it now. I can't live under the shadow of doubt—it's not fair on either of us.'

And for once there weren't any questions that needed answers. Everything Olivia needed to know was there in his eyes.

She took a tentative step off the cliff edge she had been balancing on for so long. Away from the uncertainty of the past and into the future.

'I don't need time to think about it.'

The jury was back; the verdict was in.

He stood there quite still, and she saw the apprehension in his eyes disappear as she held out her hands to him. In a second she was in his arms where she belonged, where she felt safe and loved. Whatever the future held, it would be with Clem beside her to share in the good times and catch her when she fell.

His strong arms pulled her into his ever-loving embrace and his mouth, tentatively at first, met hers, and then he kissed her with such a depth and passion she thought he might never stop. Delighting in each other's touch, neither heard as Sister Jay entered. She coughed loudly and Clem reluctantly let Olivia go.

'I didn't realise you still had visitors,' she said in a proprietorial voice. 'Miss Morrell should really be resting.'

Clem stood up like a scolded schoolboy.

'I've just had a call from Admin,' Sister Jay continued. 'It would seem there's some mix-up with your paperwork

With your next of kin being in England, whom should we put as your emergency contact?'

Olivia caught the glimpse of mischief in the elderly woman's eyes and turned her face to Clem as he sat back on the bed beside her.

'That would be me, Sister,' he said, taking Olivia's hands. 'Dr Jake Clemson, Ms Morrell's fiancé, assuming, of course, that she'll have me.'

Olivia, suddenly oblivious of their audience, answered him with a kiss.

Leaving them to it, Sister Jay gently closed the door and, sitting at her desk, started to fill in the form.

'Well?' said Hannah impatiently to her senior.

With a smile Sister Jay put down her pen. 'I think we can take it as a yes.'

MILLS & BOON®

Makes any time special™

Mills & Boon publish 29 new titles every month. Select from...

Modern Romance™   Tender Romance™

Sensual Romance™

Medical Romance™   Historical Romance™

MAT2

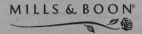

Medical Romance™

EMOTIONAL RESCUE *by Alison Roberts*

Newly qualified ambulance officer Hannah Duncan soon realises that she loves her job – and her colleague Adam Lewis! But he doesn't want children, and Hannah already has a toddler of her own. Will she be able to help rescue Adam from the demons of his past and give them all a future?

THE SURGEON'S DILEMMA *by Laura MacDonald*

Catherine Slade knew she was deeply attracted to her boss, the charismatic senior consultant Paul Grantham. She also knew he had a secret sorrow that she could help him with. If only a relationship between them wasn't so forbidden…

A FULL RECOVERY *by Gill Sanderson*

Book two of Nursing Sisters duo

If he is to persuade emotionally bruised theatre nurse Jo to love again, neurologist Ben Franklin must give her tenderness and patience. But when she does eventually give herself to him, how can he be sure she's not just on the rebound?

On sale 3rd August 2001

Available at most branches of WH Smith, Tesco, Martins, Borders, Easons, Sainsbury, Woolworth and most good paperback bookshops

0701/03a

A Perfect Family

An enthralling family saga by bestselling author

PENNY JORDAN

Published 20th July

4 FREE books and a surprise gift!

We would like to take this opportunity to thank you for reading this Mills & Boon® book by offering you the chance to take FOUR more specially selected titles from the Medical Romance™ series absolutely FREE! We're also making this offer to introduce you to the benefits of the Reader Service™—

★ FREE home delivery
★ FREE gifts and competitions
★ FREE monthly Newsletter
★ Exclusive Reader Service discounts
★ Books available before they're in the shops

Accepting these FREE books and gift places you under no obligation to buy, you may cancel at any time, even after receiving your free shipment. Simply complete your details below and return the entire page to the address below. *You don't even need a stamp!*

YES! Please send me 4 free Medical Romance books and a surprise gift. I understand that unless you hear from me, I will receive 6 superb new titles every month for just £2.49 each, postage and packing free. I am under no obligation to purchase any books and may cancel my subscription at any time. The free books and gift will be mine to keep in any case.

M1ZEA

Ms/Mrs/Miss/Mr ....Initials................................
BLOCK CAPITALS PLEASE

Surname ....

Address ....

....

....Postcode ....

Send this whole page to:
UK: FREEPOST CN81, Croydon, CR9 3WZ
EIRE: PO Box 4546, Kilcock, County Kildare (stamp required)